SINK OR SWIM

ALSO BY STEVE WATKINS

SINK
OR
SWIM

STEVE WATKINS

Scholastic Inc.

Copyright © 2017 by Steve Watkins

This book was originally published in hardcover by Scholastic Press in 2017.

All rights reserved. Published by Scholastic Inc., *Publishers since 1920.* SCHOLASTIC and associated logos are trademarks and/or registered trademarks of Scholastic Inc.

The publisher does not have any control over and does not assume any responsibility for author or third-party websites or their content.

No part of this publication may be reproduced, stored in a retrieval system, or transmitted in any form or by any means, electronic, mechanical, photocopying, recording, or otherwise, without written permission of the publisher. For information regarding permission, write to Scholastic Inc., Attention: Permissions Department, 557 Broadway, New York, NY 10012.

While inspired by real events and historical characters, this is a work of fiction and does not claim to be historically accurate or portray factual events or relationships. Please keep in mind that references to actual persons, living or dead, business establishments, events, or locales may not be factually accurate, but rather fictionalized by the author.

ISBN 978-1-338-05793-5

10 9 8 7 6 5 4 3 2 1   19 20 21 22 23

Printed in the U.S.A.   40

This edition first printing 2019

Book design by Maeve Norton

FOR WAYNE, JO, AND ORIGINAL JO

CHAPTER 1

My hands were freezing from the choppy waves in the January Atlantic Ocean. We were a mile out from Ocracoke Island off the North Carolina coast, and I had on a pair of my dad's old work gloves. My older brother, Danny, and I were there after school to do some net fishing, and it was time to let out the drop net between our two boats.

"Okay, Colton," he yelled over the rumble of both of our motors. "You got your side tied on?"

"Just about," I yelled back. "It's hard with these gloves on."

"Then take them off!" he said.

I did, and by the time I got my end of the net tied my hands were numb.

"Now run your skiff at the same speed as mine," Danny said, gesturing to my boat. "Not too fast and not too slow."

We were trawling for trout, sea bass, bluefish, whatever we lucked into, hoping for a decent catch so we could head back to shore soon, before it got too late in the afternoon and before the wind picked up and the water got nasty. It used to be the family business, but now Danny just went out when he could to help Mama with the extra money he earned from selling whatever he caught. We needed all the extra money possible after Dad died. It was hard for Mama to pay the bills when the only money coming in was from her working at the post office and washing clothes for people.

Danny was seventeen and I was twelve, so, of course, I did everything he told me, even though I was big for my age and nearly his same size. Sometimes strangers thought we were twins if they didn't look at us too close—not that we saw many strangers on the island.

It was only the third time Danny had let me come help him trawl, and there was still plenty I kept forgetting. Naturally, Danny was happy to point that out. Dad used to take Danny out on the ocean to net fish when Danny was my age, which was how he learned, but Dad passed away four years ago, before I was old enough.

When I was little, Danny was my best friend, even though he was so much older. We were always playing games around the house, going body surfing, riding beach ponies. But after Dad died, Danny didn't have much time for me anymore, or that was what he said. And I guess it was true, because he was always going straight from school to do whatever odd job he could find in town, or else out on the ocean fishing.

After we lost Dad, Danny just felt like he had to make up for it somehow. Like he had to step in to help keep the roof over our heads. And that also meant no more playing with his little brother, no matter how much I begged him to.

But in one more week, it was just going to be me doing the fishing—well, me and this kid Dean Shepherd from school who also came from a fishing family—because Danny was leaving for the navy. He'd signed up right after the Japanese attacked Pearl Harbor last month. Our navy had been getting kicked around in the South Pacific Ocean ever since then and now we heard the Germans had started attacking American ships up north that were crossing over to England. Danny wanted to do his part to fight back, especially now that the Germans and the Italians had also declared war on the US. Plus the navy pay would help out the family.

"Keep your mind on what you're doing!" Danny barked. "You're steering too close to me."

I straightened my skiff. "Sorry," I said.

He frowned. "Sorry won't help if you run into my boat, or run over the net and tear it up with your propeller."

I said sorry again, and this time tried to pay better attention to what I was doing.

We kept nosing forward together through two-foot waves, and pretty soon I felt something pull on the net, hopefully a school of fish. Danny must have felt it, too, because he gave me a thumbs-up and grinned and that made me feel better.

It was the middle of the afternoon, but no sun. Just sky so gray it could have been dusk already. We were used to it, though. I got out a harmonica that Mama had given me for my Christmas present. I was still learning how to play it. About the only song I sort of knew was "The Yellow Rose of Texas." As soon as I started, Danny groaned.

"You're not gonna play that again, are you? I must have heard it a thousand times already. Don't you know anything else? Besides, you're scaring the fish."

"I am not," I said. "Fish like music. I think."

I was about to say something else, but suddenly we heard a roaring noise from out of nowhere coming up behind us. Before we could even turn to look, a giant swell lifted our boats! He grabbed the sides. "Colton!" he yelled, but whatever he was going to say, he didn't get to finish, because the swell passed and his boat slammed down hard in the water, sending him sprawling. Something had hold of the net and jerked us both forward, like maybe a whale had gotten caught down there.

"Cut the net!" Danny yelled as we were dragged behind the swell, our boats bucking wildly, threatening to throw us out. I had a tight hold on the sides of my boat and was scared to let go to cut the net or do anything else.

Danny kept yelling, pulling out his knife and slashing at where the net was tied to his gunwale. "Cut it now, Colton!"

Just as he said it, though, the bow of his boat tipped under the surface, and he dropped his knife. Water poured over the bow and over Danny. His whole boat was going under. Panicked, I lurched forward, fumbling frantically for my knife, and somehow managed to slash through the taut ropes—just as I was about to be swallowed, too.

"I'm loose!" I hollered to Danny, only he wasn't there

anymore. His boat wasn't. The net wasn't. Nothing was, except the swell, pulling away fast.

"Danny!" I yelled as loud as I could, over and over. "Danny, where are you?"

But he was gone.

I sat there, paralyzed, rocking in the waves. The motor had quit on me, but I didn't try to start it up. I was too much in shock, staring at the place where Danny had vanished.

Then, a quarter mile ahead of my now drifting boat, something broke the surface. It was the swell giving way to something enormous and gray, only it wasn't a whale. It had a tower and deck guns, and as it kept rising out of the water, slowing down, I saw the deck, and the sides with some lettering and some numbers that were too far away for me to read.

A hatch opened and men climbed out onto the deck.

I knew what it was right away and terror froze me in place. We'd learned about it from Mrs. Payne, my seventh-grade teacher: a submarine. And not just any sub, but a German U-boat.

There was talk about Hitler's U-boats off the East Coast. Folks had been saying it was just a matter of time before there would be fighting in the Atlantic against them. Still, I could hardly believe my eyes.

I squinted into the distance and saw the fishing net and Danny's boat caught up on the bow of the U-boat, dangling over the side.

Some of the German submariners looked back in my direction, just standing around and smoking. Others went over to the boat to cut it loose and dump it into the ocean. There was still no sign of Danny anywhere.

One of the men pointed at me and seemed to be laughing, though I couldn't hear anything except the groaning ocean and waves slapping the sides of my boat. Some other men joined the laughing submariner. Others just stood there.

I was still so scared that I couldn't move. There was no place to go anyway. Nowhere to hide. I couldn't jump in the water or I'd freeze. My motor was still stalled out, and I doubted I could get it started quickly enough to get away. And even if I managed, I knew I couldn't outrun those deck guns.

They didn't do anything, though, except eventually go back down below, close the hatch, and churn away through the dark Atlantic until the sub was just a speck on the horizon.

I did the best I could to shake off being paralyzed from fear. I had to find Danny. So I got busy trying to start up the motor, praying it would still work. And like a miracle, it did. I was taking on water through a crack in the hull, but I couldn't worry about that now. I aimed for the spot where the U-boat had surfaced, hoping I'd find Danny, calling his name again, over and over.

Ten minutes later I saw him, his head barely above the waterline, clutching the ice box where we stored the fish we caught. I forgot about where that U-boat might be lurking. "Danny!" I yelled. "Hold on!"

He didn't lift his head or say anything when I pulled up beside him, but at least he was still breathing. He'd probably used all the strength he had clinging on to the ice box. I could barely peel his fingers off to loosen his grip, and then hang on to his arm to keep him from slipping under. The ice box bobbed away out of reach.

I wasn't big enough or strong enough to just pull Danny in, so I had to figure something out—and fast, before he got hypothermia and died. Then I could deal with whatever injuries he might have had from being lifted and slammed and dragged underwater by the U-boat.

I grabbed a line from the bottom of my boat and looped it around the arm I was holding, pulling him up with it as far as I could, and then tying it off. I did the same with more rope and one of Danny's legs. Then, with him secured to the side of my boat, I reached for Danny's belt, took hold, braced my feet against the hull, and pulled with all my might until I got him up to the side—and then over. He landed on top of me, both of us splashing into a couple of inches of oily water.

I sat Danny up as best I could and wrapped a tarp around him because it was about the only thing I had to try to keep him warm. "Just hold on," I told him, even though he was still unconscious. "Don't die!"

Once I had him situated, I aimed the boat back toward Ocracoke—actually north of the island a little way, since the currents would be pulling me south and I had to account for that. I tied off the throttle to keep it open as fast as the waves would let me, and then spent the next half hour bailing water with an old coffee can.

Danny moaned a couple of times but didn't open his eyes. Once I had enough water out that the boat could ride high enough to make decent time, I went over to check him, feel for broken bones or anything I could think of. But whatever was wrong with him, I didn't know enough to be able to tell. Maybe he hit his head, though I couldn't feel a lump. Maybe he had water in his lungs. Maybe something inside was broken or torn.

"Hang on, Danny," I whispered to him, hugging him partly to try to make him warmer, and partly—mostly—because I was so scared and wished he would wake up and tell me what else I should do that I hadn't thought of yet. I started crying, which I hadn't done since Dad died. Thankfully, there wasn't anybody around to see me doing it—especially nobody from school—and if by some other miracle Danny was to open his eyes just then, I doubted he'd make fun of me under the circumstances.

It was growing darker, which turned out to be not such a bad thing because now I could see lights on the island and had something to navigate to. But I still hated, hated, hated being out on the ocean in the nighttime.

CHAPTER 2

Mama was waiting for us on the beach, something she always did whenever we went fishing, though we were hours late this time. I saw a lantern first, and then her, standing right where she knew we would put to shore. She had her jeans rolled up and a flannel shirt on but nothing else, not even a hat. And she waded out to take hold of the bow before we even made it all the way in. Her tanned face looked white in the glow of the lantern.

"What happened?" she said as she grabbed Danny's arm and felt his pulse. She didn't wait for me to answer before she lifted him half out of the boat and then told me to take his legs and help her get him up on the sand.

I was crying too hard to answer. I knew Danny needed help, but I wanted Mama to take me in her arms and hug me and tell me everything was going to be okay and not to worry. But instead she said, "You can't cry right now, Colton. You need to quickly tell me what happened and then run up to town to get help. Danny needs you to be strong for a few more minutes."

I swallowed hard and managed to say, "Yes, Mama," and then I blurted out that there was a German U-boat and it sank Danny's boat and I lost sight of Danny and he went under and I didn't know how long and I was so scared but I found him and it took me forever to get back to the island and I kept him as warm as I could and—

Mama stopped me. She was all business. "That's enough for now, Colton. Run as fast as you can to get help. Go get Dr. Evans and then Officer Winslow."

I took off, running as hard as I could, my feet digging into the sand and feeling like lead. I was so out of breath when I got to Dr. Evans that he tried to make me lie down. But I waved him off. "It's my brother! We need help!"

I started to explain what happened, but I probably didn't make much sense. Dr. Evans grabbed his black medical bag and told me I could tell him the rest later, but right now

I had to go get the one policeman on the island, Officer Winslow. Then he took off for the beach, moving a lot faster than I thought a man as heavy as him could.

Mama was still holding Danny in her lap when Officer Winslow and I got there, using her body to keep him as warm as she could, the damp tarp pulled over both of them. Dr. Evans was checking Danny for broken bones.

"There's a head injury, but that's about all I know right now," he said. "We need to get him up to the clinic right away and warm him up from this hypothermia."

We used the tarp for a stretcher to carry him up to the clinic—each one of us lifting a corner, me struggling the hardest because I was the smallest. Mama filled them in from what little I'd told her, but she was calm enough that at least they could understand what she was saying. I was still panting too hard to add anything more until a lot later, after we got Danny to the clinic, cleaned up, out of his wet clothes, and under warm blankets, with an IV line in his arm for fluids.

I did my best to tell them the whole story while Dr. Evans checked Danny again for any broken bones he might have missed, listened to his breathing with his stethoscope, and checked his vital signs.

Finally, when I finished, Mama hugged me. "You were mighty brave out there, Colton," she said.

And then she turned her attention back to Danny. We all did, even though there was nothing anybody could do except wait for him to wake up.

"Is he in a coma, Dr. Evans?" Mama asked. I swallowed hard at the thought.

"It's too early to say, Mrs. Graham," Dr. Evans replied.

"Well, if it isn't a coma, then what is it?" Mama asked. I could hear the steel in her voice, but I also realized Mama must be scared, too. She was trying not to let it show.

"I don't know for sure," Dr. Evans said. "I mean, he's unconscious, but it could be that once he warms up enough, and once we get enough fluids in him, he'll be just fine."

The way he said it, though, not looking at Mama when he talked, made me think Danny really was in a coma, but Dr. Evans didn't want to say it. Even I knew that if you're just unconscious, you'll wake up eventually, but if you're in a coma, you might never wake up.

We stayed there with Danny all night. Mama mostly prayed, or leaned over Danny and whispered in his ear in a voice too low for me to hear. And probably too far away for Danny to hear. But she kept trying.

Dr. Evans left after a couple of hours but came back first thing in the morning. He was the only doctor on the island and always had a lot of folks to see. He came into Danny's room first, though. There wasn't any change.

"I don't think it's a good idea to try to move him to the mainland just yet," he said. Officer Winslow had come back, too, and he chimed in that with a U-boat out there, nobody was too keen on the idea of launching a boat across the sound to take Danny anywhere anyway.

Mama didn't say anything. She hadn't slept and had really dark circles around her eyes.

Mrs. Thorson, the nurse, brought Mama some coffee and we sat in silence while she drank it.

And we waited. One day, two days, a week.

I slept in two chairs pulled together next to Danny's bed and only ever left to go to the bathroom. I *tried* to sleep anyway. Except whenever I closed my eyes I kept hearing that roar behind us and seeing that swell come up under us, and Danny disappearing, and those German U-boat sailors standing on their deck, cutting loose Danny's boat and smoking their cigarettes and looking back at me like none of it mattered. Like Danny and I were nothing to them. Not even real people.

I woke up sweating even though it was cold in the clinic. The winter wind was picking up outside, the loud surf half a mile away sounding like it was hitting up against the other side of the wall.

Mama was there as much as she could be, sitting with Danny and me, but with her two jobs, she kept having to leave. After the first few days of Danny being in the coma—eventually even Dr. Evans started calling it that— she got on me that I had to go to school, but I wouldn't do it. I felt like what had happened to him was my fault somehow.

And with money already tight, now it was going to be even tighter. No money from Danny's fishing. No money from him going into the navy. Instead, his being in the hospital was just going to mean more bills.

I told Mama I thought I should drop out of school and see about getting a job on one of the trawlers that operated on the island. Or get with Dean Shepherd after school and go out every afternoon with the drop net to catch our own fish like Danny did, not just once in a while like I'd originally figured.

Mama hugged me when I told her that. "Absolutely not," she said. "Your job right now is to go to school and learn.

You can help out in the afternoons like you planned, but you're too young to do more than that. We'll figure this out. We always do."

I really didn't see how we'd be okay this time. I started to protest, but she interrupted me. "It's not your fault, Colton," she said. "It's not anybody's fault except the Germans on that submarine. And that horrible man." She practically spit the name "Hitler," and her face darkened when she said it.

"That's whose fault it really is," she continued, as if she knew him—and hated him—personally.

I hated Hitler, too. I hated all of the Nazis and wished I had done something, anything, when I had the chance. Maybe I could have started my motor and attacked them. Got close enough to throw my knife at them. Rammed their U-boat with the dinghy and done some kind of damage to something.

But I'd just sat there, scared.

Mama finally talked me into going home. "You need to change your clothes, take a bath, and get a good night's sleep," she said. "Then you can come back."

It was the middle of January and already getting dark. I'd been sitting so long that my legs felt weak when Mama and I stepped outside the clinic and stumbled down the street.

I'd walked here a million times before, but now everything was different somehow. Ocracoke had always seemed so safe. The ocean could be terrible sometimes, but the island was always something you could take for granted. Only now I kept looking around as if I was expecting Hitler himself to just show up with his Nazis to take over the island.

We didn't even make it a block, to the Methodist church, when suddenly there was an explosion out on the ocean. At first we couldn't see anything except a sudden red sky, but we felt it.

Everybody stopped dead in their tracks, right in the middle of the street, cars and everything, then they all started talking at once, wondering what that could have been, miles out on the ocean somewhere south of the island. In the back of everybody's mind was the same thing, though, and in an hour we knew it was true. U-boats had sunk a freighter called the *Allan Jackson* down at Oregon Inlet. Every fishing boat available was rushing out to search for survivors.

I never did end up going home, even when Mama ordered me to again. I turned around and went back to the clinic to be with Danny. If I couldn't help on the water, I might as well be with my brother. As I walked, I saw people dashing about dimming lights, pulling the shades tight, nailing up blankets, and doing whatever else so the whole island could make itself safe by disappearing into the dark.

We'd only had electricity on Ocracoke for about three years. Goats on the island had long ago eaten up just about all the vegetation, so there was nothing to block anybody lurking out on the ocean from seeing every lit-up house and building and car and boat and dock and barn at night. But without anyone talking about it, the whole island either turned off their lights or blacked out the windows. Even the clinic was dark by the time I returned.

In the dim room with Danny I leaned close to his ear, so mad at Hitler and the U-boats and the Germans that I trembled the whole time, and I made him a promise. "I'm going to get them back, Danny. I don't know how, and I don't know what it's going to take, but I swear I'm going to do it."

The next day, we found out there weren't any survivors from the *Allan Jackson*. Just oil and debris washed up on shore. And then the following day, the U-boats sank another cargo ship, the *City of Atlanta*, seven miles off the North Carolina coast.

Only three out of forty-six survived that torpedo attack.

The Coast Guard put a call out for anybody with a big enough boat to volunteer for U-boat patrol duty. Everybody agreed it was crazy, since no fishing boat had any sort of gun on it, and no shark rifle would do damage to a submarine. But they figured we had to do something while we waited for the navy to send help. Maybe if a fishing boat spotted a sub and radioed any cargo ships in the area to warn them, they could take evasive action, change course, do something to save themselves.

And I kind of understood why folks might want to help, even if it was crazy. Because as scared as I was about the Germans attacking us, I was also mad. Mad that they were invading and mad about what they'd done to Danny.

So once I heard about the call, I finally left Danny and went down to the docks to see Mr. Jenkins, an old friend of Dad's, who I knew had the biggest shrimp trawler on Ocracoke. I figured he had to be going out to look for subs, and I was determined to get him to take me with him.

He took one look at me when I asked, though, and just shook his head. "Son, your mama needs you here, and your brother needs you here, and if I let you go out on my boat, the ghost of your dad would come down and put a haunt on me sure as anything."

We were in a small tin shed that Mr. Jenkins used for an office and for storing stuff, or just to hang out when he didn't want to go home, which was a lot of the time because his wife took in stray cats and Mr. Jenkins hated cats and said the whole house smelled of cat business and he couldn't stand it.

So he sat in his little shed when he wasn't out on the water, and he smoked a pipe like Dad used to do, and ate cheese and sardines from a can on saltine crackers with mustard, and washed it down with warm beer.

He offered me some—the crackers and all, but not the beer—and my stomach rumbled since I'd hardly eaten all week because I'd been so worried about Danny. I sat on a barrel next to Mr. Jenkins and wolfed down a whole pack of crackers piled high with cheese and sardines, though I said "No thank you" to the mustard.

"You know, Colton," Mr. Jenkins said after a long silence, broken only by the sounds of us eating and the occasional boat leaving the docks. "There's going to be a lot of our boys going out on patrols and not coming back. Brave or foolish, or both, they're heading out there thinking they're going to sink 'em a U-boat with a peashooter. 'Cept it ain't going to happen."

"But you're going, aren't you?" I asked, sure that Mr. Jenkins was. Dad told me Mr. Jenkins had been a soldier in the Great War, and he'd been in trenches in France that got poison gas exploded on them, which was why he had a gaspy way of breathing all the time.

Mr. Jenkins shrugged. "You do what you got to do. I got a big enough boat. Maybe it'll scare 'em away. Meanwhile, you're needed on land. I sure am sorry about your brother. I been praying for him to get better, and I have faith he will. Just going to take some time is all."

I wanted to believe him, but now that another week had passed, and Danny was still in a coma, I was starting to lose hope. If only Danny had left a week earlier for Raleigh, the North Carolina capital, where he was supposed to report for duty, none of this would have ever happened. He'd have already been on a bus from the navy recruitment office up to the Great Lakes naval training center in Illinois to do his basic training on Lake Michigan.

I thanked Mr. Jenkins for the cheese and crackers and all, wiped my hands—oily from the sardines—on my jeans, and headed back to the clinic.

On the way there I thought about Mama, about how she hadn't cried once since meeting us on the beach when I came in that night with Danny. The closest she'd come was one night when I fell asleep in the chairs in Danny's room, and I woke up to see Mama sitting so close to Danny that she was practically on the bed, her hands clenched tight together and her eyes squeezed shut. She was praying—whispering so I couldn't hear, but I still knew—and drops of water rolled down her cheeks but it wasn't tears. It was Mama praying so hard she was sweating.

I didn't think Mama had cried since Dad died, and I knew she wasn't going to start now. She was going to believe Danny would get better, and she was going to pray that it would be so, and she was going to go to work every day and take care of us.

I also knew, thinking about all that, that I had to do something to help, and it wasn't just going to be sitting around by Danny's bed waiting for him to wake up out of that coma. Since he wasn't bringing in any money now, it was up to me to do it, just like Danny had been the one to step up after we lost Dad. That's the way it was in our family and on the island.

More than anything I just wanted to be a kid, though. To go back to school and play baseball with Dean Shepherd and my other friends, and ride my beach pony, and play checkers with Mama when she wasn't too tired from working, and talk to this girl Denise Olsen who was in my Sunday School class and who I kind of liked but wasn't going to admit it to anybody, especially her.

But it was my turn to help our family, and halfway back to the clinic I stopped. Because it just hit me how I was going to do it—this crazy idea that left me out of breath just thinking it.

Why didn't I take Danny's recruitment papers and his identification and get to Raleigh? I could join up as him. Everybody said we looked alike and that I was big for my age. I didn't shave, and I didn't have much hair in places you're supposed to get hair, but maybe they wouldn't check down there. Maybe I could wear some of Danny's clothes and a hat pulled down low on my face so they couldn't see me too well. And make myself all dirty, like I just came from working on a farm or something. You always looked older when you were wearing a hat, and when you had dirt on you. And I'd wear boots so I was taller, too.

And if they let me in, and if they sent me to the Naval Training Center Great Lakes, and if I got through that, then maybe, just maybe, they'd put me on a ship in the Atlantic and I'd chase down every last one of Hitler's U-boats and sink them to the bottom of the sea.

I went back down to the ocean instead of to the clinic and sat on a high sand dune and stared out at the Atlantic. Hours went by while I thought over what I was considering doing. It was crazy. And it probably wouldn't work. And I'd probably just get found out and sent back home. And if it did work, wouldn't I be so scared and homesick that I'd crack being so far away and by myself? Would I even be able to make it through basic training? I'd never been farther away from Ocracoke than Morehead City, and I was just five years old that time and got lost, and when they found me I was standing in the middle of a street bawling my eyes out. What made me think I could handle leaving the island to join the navy?

In the end, though, it felt like there wasn't really even a choice to make. In our family, you stepped up when you had to. Danny did it. Mama did it. And now it was my turn.

Scared to death as I might be, I was going.

CHAPTER 3

If I was going to go, I had to do it today. Otherwise, I might not make it to Raleigh in time. It would be another hour before Mama got home, so I didn't have long to write a note and pack.

> *Dear Mama,*
>
> *I'm sorry but I can't wait here anymore for Danny to wake up from his coma. I know he will one day, but in the meantime I have to do something, and since I can't take the boats out with him anymore to fish, and since nobody's doing any fishing anyway with those U-boats out there, I'm going over to Morehead City to find a job to make some money to send back to you.*

There aren't any jobs on the island—not even any tourists are going to come over when it's summer, I bet—and I don't have it in me to go back to school right now. I feel so awful about what happened to Danny that I hate even being on the island anymore, to tell you the honest truth. I expect that will change once he wakes up and is okay, but for now this is the best plan I can come up with. I will send money soon and write to let you know that I am okay. Don't worry about me. Dad was my age when he went to work, and it's time for me to do my part to help out. I love you and Danny.

Your son, Colton

Of course, I wasn't really going to Morehead City—that was just to make Mama think I was. I felt bad about lying to her, but I couldn't tell her the truth or she'd come right away and find me, or contact the navy and they'd send me right back home.

I had all of Danny's recruitment papers wrapped up safe in the bottom of a canvas sack with some of his clothes. I wouldn't need much. Danny had told me you just showed up at the recruiters with the clothes on your back and they even take those away when you get to the Naval Training Center Great Lakes and give you your uniforms, and from then on you belong to the navy and do what they tell you and wear what they tell you, even down to your underwear and shoes.

I headed over to the sound side and got into the dinghy and navigated through choppy water across the Pamlico Sound to a little fishing town called Oriental. My plan was to stash the boat there and hitchhike to Raleigh, even though I hadn't ever hitchhiked before. I figured it was just like they said—you stood by the road, stuck out your thumb, and when somebody stopped, you told them where you were going.

It was nighttime when I got to Oriental. And it was bitter cold and had been for hours during the crossing. I wanted to find someplace to eat and a warm place to sleep, except I didn't have but a couple of dollars to my name. So I dragged the dinghy high up on shore, flipped it over, crawled under, and spent the night shivering, wearing Danny's heaviest coat with a tarp pulled over me.

I barely slept—mostly I just lay there and cried, then got mad at myself for crying and made myself stop until I got so scared again that the tears started back up. I thought about when Mama told me there wasn't time for me to be crying, that I needed to tell her what happened and then go get help for Danny. And I told myself that that's what I was doing and why I couldn't cry anymore—because I was going to go get help for Danny and Mama by doing what I was doing. And that's pretty much how it went all night long. I'd get scared, almost start to cry, tell myself those things again, and maybe fall asleep for a little while, but then wake up shivering and start all over again. I just hoped they wouldn't ask me too many questions in Raleigh, or look me over too close, or laugh at me and tell me to go home. In the darkest hours of the night, the thing that got me through—and got me up the next morning, and got me out on the highway to thumb down my first ride—was remembering the other reason why I was doing all this: to be a subchaser and make them pay for what they did to Danny.

I got lucky on my first ride, because it was a preacher in a Rambler going all the way to Durham, which was the other side of Raleigh, so I figured I would be able to lean back and catch up on all the sleep I didn't get the night before, with that Rambler's heater warming me up so I could feel my fingers and toes again.

My luck ran out pretty quick, though, because it looked like that preacher expected me to have a conversation with him the whole way there, and most of that conversation was him trying to save my soul, even though I kept telling him my soul had already been saved by the Methodist Church.

Eventually, he stopped for gas and offered to buy me a cup of coffee and a sandwich, and I was grateful enough to put up with his preaching for another couple of hours.

"That's mighty nice of you," I said about the sandwich and coffee, and he must have liked that I said it because he bought me a giant pickle from a pickle barrel they had in the store there at the gas pumps. He warned me not to drip any on the front seat of his Rambler because he liked to keep his car neat and clean the way the good Lord intended.

I didn't know anything about that but did promise to be careful with that pickle.

We finally made it to Raleigh.

"Well, thank you, sir," I said as he slowed the car down.

It was only when he pulled over and turned to me that I think it occurred to him how young I might've been. "Son, are you a runaway? Or are you in any kind of trouble?"

"No, sir," I said. "I'm joining the navy. I'm going to fight the Germans."

He looked at me with a funny expression. "Why, you're just a boy. How are you joining the navy?"

I sat up as tall as I could. "I'm seventeen," I said, trying to keep my voice from cracking, something it had been doing a lot of lately.

The preacher shook his head sadly. "I'll be praying for you."

"Thank you. If you could also pray for my brother, I'd appreciate it," I said. I figured he *was* a preacher and must've known how to say a lot better prayer than somebody like me.

"He younger or older?" the preacher asked.

I thought about it, then decided since I was pretending to be Danny, I should probably pretend Danny was me. "He's my kid brother," I said. "His name is Colton. We were out fishing and one of those German subs ran into us and he got hurt pretty bad. He's in a coma."

The preacher shook his head again. "Sorry to hear that. I'll pray that the Lord looks after him. And looks after you, too. We're all going to need His help, I reckon. There's an awful big storm coming."

I thought about that U-boat and the attacks on those first two ships.

That awful big storm wasn't just coming. It was already here.

CHAPTER 4

I was real worried that they'd have doctors at the recruit-ment center in Raleigh doing physical exams and they'd know I wasn't as old as I pretended to be. And I was real worried that they'd have a dentist there, too, and they'd see that I still had a couple of baby teeth, and so couldn't really be seventeen. And I was real worried that even with dirt streaked on my face, Dad's old wool cap pulled low on my forehead, Danny's baggy clothes, my boots on to make me taller, and the way I'd been practicing making my voice lower like a grown man's that they'd see through my disguise and toss me out.

But none of that happened. There were so many of us crammed into the recruitment office to report for boot camp that they just read off a list of our names and everybody said "Here" or "Present" or "Yeah" and that was it.

"So they don't have a doctor do an exam or anything?" I asked the guy next to me, who didn't seem a whole lot older than I was.

"Guess not," he said. "Got my exam before, when I first come in to enlist. They didn't do that for you?"

"Oh yeah," I said, covering. "I just didn't know if we'd get another one here."

"All right, all right, all right!" A navy officer stormed into the room just then and barked at us. "We're still waiting on a couple of stragglers. The rest of you hit the head out back, and then line up outside and get on the bus, and keep your yaps shut while you're doing it."

I'd been on enough boats in my life to know that the *head* was the bathroom, so I got in line to take care of business and then spent the next three hours just sitting on the bus outside the recruitment office, not going anywhere, and nobody telling us why. When I finally said something about it to the guy sitting next to me—the same guy as before— he replied, "I heard it was gonna be like this. Hurry up and wait. I guess it's our official welcome to the navy."

I nodded like I knew what he was talking about.

"Name's Woody Hudson, by the way," he said.

"Colt—" I started to say before I caught myself. "I mean, Danny."

Woody gave me a funny look, and I was nervous I'd already blown it and we hadn't even left Raleigh yet. "I go by Danny," I tried to clarify.

"All right, Danny it is," Woody said with a laugh. "Where you from anyway, Danny?"

"Outer Banks. What about you?"

He said he was from Kinston, which was a farming town east of Raleigh I'd heard of. Then he leaned in close. "I ain't but fifteen," he said. "And I ain't never been out of Kinston before, neither. I thought they'd know when I come over last month to the recruitment office, but they just let me sign up. My ma, she signed the papers. She didn't care I wasn't seventeen yet and didn't mind telling them I was, neither. The way I see it, the navy's gonna put some money in my pocket and I can do what I want from now on."

I said that seemed like a funny way to think about it, since you had to follow orders in the navy, but he just laughed again. "Ain't you never heard of liberty? That's when you get a pass and they let you off the ship or off the base or wherever you're at, and you can go out and drink and watch movies and see if you can find you a girl. All kinds of things you can do if you got money."

Woody had sandy hair and was a couple of inches taller than me—I was five foot six on tiptoes and had a thick mop of black hair like Danny and Dad. Woody was also a big talker. Once he finished up with all the wild stuff he was going to do when he had that money in his pocket and was on liberty, he started in on everything anybody might ever want to know about growing and cropping and curing tobacco. Then after that he told me all about his high school and the teachers there, and the sports teams he'd been on, and all the girls who did or didn't talk to him, and who he would or wouldn't go out on a date with, and who was or wasn't pretty enough for him. Woody kept on talking for a good half hour. The best I could figure out, Woody hadn't ever actually been out with a girl, but he did have a lot of big plans.

I didn't mind him going on and on like that, though. I didn't want anybody asking me any questions, and listening to Woody helped keep my mind off all the things I was worrying about—like Danny and Mama and getting caught.

Without us noticing, the stragglers must have shown up, because right about the time I was going to ask if I could get off and use the head again, the doors slammed shut and the bus jerked into gear and off we went up the highway for the twenty-hour drive to the boot camp at Great Lakes, where they would turn us all into proper sailors before sending us off to war.

Anybody on the bus who'd brought food shared it with the rest of us, which was a good thing for me because I hadn't eaten anything since leaving Ocracoke except that sandwich and pickle and cup of coffee the preacher had bought me. Somebody had fried chicken. Somebody else had a hard salami that he cut into slices with his knife and passed around. Somebody else even had a jar of moonshine that he offered around, but I passed on that. I hadn't ever had liquor before and didn't think Mama would like it if I drank some, even though there wouldn't be a way for her to find out.

Woody took a big long drink of it, like it was no big deal, but his eyes started watering and his face got all red and he couldn't speak for about five minutes because he was gasping for air. All the older guys got a good laugh out of that, and the more they drank the more they were yelling and carrying on until the officer in charge of the bus turned on the lights and stomped up and down the aisle ordering us to pipe down or we'd regret it once we got to Great Lakes.

Once the jar was empty they passed it around again for guys to pee in, then dump it out the window and pass it to the next fellow. Somebody must have spilled some, though, or maybe the wind blew some back in the windows, because it got to smelling like pee so bad on the bus that I got a headache.

"You think this is bad," Woody said. "I heard that once you're on a ship, down below deck where the crew sleeps, it stinks to high heaven from nobody ever taking a bath and it's worse than getting seasick. More guys throw up on account of the smell than they do from their ship getting bounced around in a big storm."

"I think I'll be all right there," I said, trying to sound more confident than I actually felt. "I've been out in some rough ocean before, since I was a little kid, and never once got seasick."

"Always a first time," Woody said.

The first thing they did when we got to Great Lakes was divide up all us North Carolina boys and assign us to different companies, so we were mixed up with guys who'd come from other places all around the country—though Woody and I somehow ended up in the same company. Then they lined us up and gave us buzz cuts, so right away everybody started looking the same, which I guess was the point. The barber took one look at me after he lifted Dad's cap off my head and laughed. "You come in with your papa?"

I scowled at him with what I hoped was my meanest grown-up face, but that just made him laugh more. "Don't wet your pants, son," he said. "I just cut hair. I don't check IDs."

A minute later he was done with me and I looked just like everybody else, only apparently a lot younger. After haircuts they ordered us to strip out of the clothes we came in wearing, which we did, but then we had to stand there naked, the whole bunch of us, shivering from the Illinois cold. I found my way to a corner and covered myself up as best I could with my hands, turning away like I needed to study something on the wall behind me. Nobody seemed to notice. They were all mumbling to one another, shivering, complaining, until finally they started calling names off the recruit list. One by one we made our way to the counter where they issued us our whites and blues—the two different color uniforms we'd be wearing every day, all the way down to boots and socks and underwear, which they called skivvies. They said we could box up our civilian clothes and mail them home, but I left mine on a bench since I didn't have anywhere to send them.

I was just glad to finally be dressed again.

Next they issued us our sea bags—big canvas bags, one for each of us, that we'd use to carry everything they gave us: hammock and mattress and two mattress covers that somebody called a fart sack (I later understood why). Also one pillow and two pillow covers and a couple of blankets. A peacoat. Underwear and uniforms and not much else.

The petty officer demonstrated how we were expected to lay all our bedding items and clothes in a particular order before rolling them in the mattress so they wouldn't take up much room when we strapped it all to our sea bag. He kept calling us boots the whole time.

"All right, boots," he yelled. "That's how it's done and that's how you'll do it from now on. It's navy regulation. And everything in your life from this minute forward will be done according to navy regulations. When you eat, pee, poop, wipe yourself, tie your shoe, stand in line, even when you complain you will do it according to navy regulations. You understand me?"

"Yes, sir," I said, before I could stop myself. But I'd always been raised to say "Yes, sir" and "No, sir," so it was just a habit. No one else had spoken, though, and I realized it wasn't the sort of question that we were supposed to answer.

The petty officer glared at me but let it go. It was the last time anybody would let anything go for the next six weeks.

CHAPTER 5

I'd slept some on the bus, though not as much as I'd have liked, with Woody yakking away most of the time, and all the other guys carrying on, even after the officer stormed around and ordered them to knock it off. So when my head hit my pillow that night at Great Lakes I didn't have time to be homesick or anything—I just conked right out. I would have stayed asleep for a week, except that at five in the morning somebody came into our barracks hammering on a metal trash can lid and yelling: "You have five minutes to square your bunk, get into your blues, hit the head, and assemble! Five minutes!"

It took me forever to untangle myself from my blankets and then not step on anybody below me as I dropped to the floor and scrambled to get dressed. Woody didn't budge, so I shook him and told him to get up before he got in trouble, but he just rolled over and pulled a blanket over his head.

I was late getting to the head so there was already a line of guys waiting to pee standing shoulder to shoulder into a long trough. There wasn't any privacy between the toilets, either, for those guys needing to do their business sitting down, so I skipped that, even though I had to go.

Two minutes later, we were standing at attention in a line at the foot of our bunks. Chief Petty Officer Merkel, our company commander—who we were just supposed to call Chief—was fuming. He yelled at Woody and then dumped him on the floor. He even kicked Woody in the butt, which made Woody cry.

"Are you crying, boot?" Chief yelled. "There's no crying in the navy! Who told you you could cry in my navy?"

Woody stood up and wiped his eyes and his nose and mumbled something, but Chief wasn't happy about any of it. "Did I tell you you could wipe the snot off your face? No, I did not. The navy owns that snot, and it is not up to you to decide when and where and how to wipe it. Now put it back!"

Woody blinked.

"I said put it back!" Chief yelled again.

Woody sort of reverse wiped his face, and Chief moved on to yell at somebody else for something else. Then he dumped all our sea bags on the floor and bellowed at us to redo everything and this time to do it according to those navy regulations. He kept yelling that we better know what navy regulations were since they had been explained to us last night, plus they were in our Bluejackets' Manual, which was this kind of navy bible they'd given us that they said had everything we would need to know to go from being a boot to being a trained sailor.

We repacked our sea bags twice more before Chief was satisfied, and then he ordered us out of the barracks and over to the Grinder, double time. Nobody knew what the Grinder was until he led us there, most of us already out of breath because double time was the same thing as running, and our lungs hurt from the below-freezing temperature. When we got there—the Grinder turned out to be a drill field—Chief ordered us to keep running around the perimeter. Other companies were running, too, and he pointed about a hundred yards ahead of us and said if we ever wanted to so much as *smell* breakfast we were going to pick up the pace and pass that sorry bunch.

It was hard getting enough traction on the icy ground to go much faster, and when several guys somehow managed to surge ahead, Chief barked at them to come back. "This company is only as fast as the slowest man here," he yelled, and for some reason he was looking at me when he said it, like he thought I'd be the slowest runner just because I was the shortest guy on the Grinder.

He kept yelling at us to "Move it, move it, move it!" and we all picked up the pace as best we could, but as hard as we moved it, moved it, moved it we couldn't gain any ground on the company in front of us. Every time it seemed as if we were making progress, Chief ordered us to wait for the stragglers—which I was thankful didn't include me. Some of the guys were obviously in pretty terrible shape, but I wasn't one of them.

We ran for an hour, long after the other company had peeled off and headed to the mess hall for breakfast. Continuing on was torture. I couldn't feel my fingers or toes. My nose was running the navy's snot all down my face. And every time a lap around the Grinder took us near the mess hall we could smell the bacon and eggs and coffee and toast. Our stomachs rumbled as loud as our boots on the frozen drill field.

Finally, Chief took mercy on us, or got sick of seeing us drag around the Grinder so slow, and ordered us to stop. But he kept yelling at us. "The problem as I see it is that I must have done something wrong somewhere along the way, and as punishment the navy gave me you dirtballs to train. How I'm supposed to do that is a mystery for the ages, because if you took all the brains from all the skulls in this company, they wouldn't add up to one whole entire brain. And how God Almighty was able to make a group of men—excuse me, a group of *boys*—capable of moving so ever-loving slow is another mystery for the ages."

He spit on the ground to indicate how disgusted he was with us—I bet it froze immediately—then told us to head over to the mess hall in case there was anything left, and he hoped there wasn't because as far as he was concerned we didn't deserve to eat, as pathetic a job as we'd done so far of becoming navy men.

I had the feeling that this was how Chief would be talking to us all during boot camp from now on, and the best thing I could do was follow every order and otherwise make myself invisible.

Easier said than done, of course.

* * *

The rest of the day was a blur of doing calisthenics until we couldn't stand up anymore; lying and kneeling and standing to shoot during target practice; holding our rifles over our heads while we stood at attention until we couldn't feel our arms, but every time somebody lowered their arms we had to start over. Unfortunately, it kept being me who couldn't hold my gun up—three times—and guys started giving me dirty looks and cursing at me under their breath. I felt terrible—and weak—and gritted my teeth the fourth time and told myself I would die or my arms would have to break off before I let my rifle down, and that time I was able to hold on.

After that we loaded heavy shells into a 5" cannon, then emptied the shells, then loaded them in again, over and over and over until it was automatic. I thought that would be about it for the day, but we seemed to just be getting started, because the next thing I knew we were marching over to an indoor pool the size of a small ocean and swimming back and forth across it with our clothes on—and dragging, or being dragged by, another guy.

Fortunately, it was sunny outside, because our clothes were only partly dry when we were ordered back to the Grinder for more marching drills—and getting yelled at by

Chief whenever anybody wasn't in step. Which was often, especially for Woody. He didn't seem to know his right from his left, so the guys on either side of him started punching him on one arm or the other to let him know. I felt bad for him but was glad they hadn't done that to me earlier when I had a hard time holding up my rifle.

Finally, late in the afternoon, after Woody had screwed up yet again, even with the guys pounding on his arms—or maybe because of that—Chief ordered us to halt, and we were so tired that half the company marched into the other half before they stopped. I nearly fell down but somebody—a guy who was probably twice my size—grabbed my arm and held me up.

"Hate for a boy like you to get yourself trampled out here in the Grinder," he said.

I was going to thank him for helping me, but when he called me a boy I just scowled at him—though once again, my mean grown-up face just made somebody laugh.

Once the company got itself sorted out, Chief launched into a round of loud cursing that went on for a good five minutes before he ran out of either cusswords or breath or both. "I'm going to list all the things you do not know and it will not be a comprehensive list because that would take too long, but I have to start somewhere," he shouted. Then he barked out dozens of nautical terms and ranks and regulations while we just stood there at attention and listened and tried to remember them but, of course, couldn't because there were too many.

Chief knew we were struggling, and he stopped reciting the list so he could yell at us some more about how dumb we were. "The reason you boots don't know any of this is because the *B* in B Company must stand for *babies*. There isn't a man among you, and to even call you boys is an insult to boys everywhere, so you must be babies and ought to be wearing diapers. If I had my way, I would requisition a hundred diapers right here and now and make you wear them so you didn't poop in your skivvies because you don't have enough sense to even go to the head by yourselves."

Only *poop* wasn't the word he used.

"All right, you sorry boots," Chief continued. "One more thing that I am absolutely certain of is that half of you don't even know how to tie your own shoelaces, which might help explain why you keep tripping over one another and over your own two feet. But it's my job to teach you how to tie knots, and you will learn to tie knots—nautical knots—starting with the most fundamental and important knot of all, the bowline. It is my belief that not only can none of you tie a bowline, but that none of you even knows what a bowline is!"

Chief stopped yelling and stared at us for a second, as if he was expecting an answer. And stupid me, I raised my hand.

Chief glared at me, and I knew I'd made a mistake. I quickly took my hand down, but it was too late.

"Is your arm a balloon, boot?" he demanded.

"What, Chief?" I said.

"You heard me. I don't mumble. Now is it? Is your arm a balloon, and that's why it just lifted up from your side and went up into the air like that—because your arm is a balloon?"

"No, Chief," I whispered.

"Then get your butt down on the ground and give me fifty push-ups. When I want you to raise your hand I'll tell you to raise your hand, only I'm never going to do that because it would indicate that I think you have an answer to a question I might be asking and I know for a fact that you and everybody else in this company is too dumb for that."

I got down on the ground and struggled through ten push-ups, sure there was no way I was going to be able to finish fifty. But when I slowed down, I felt his boot on my back, and when I bent my arms to lower myself he shoved me all the way onto the ground.

"Oof!" I grunted, then struggled back up.

He shoved me back down again, hard, and kept doing that until I somehow managed to do the fifty push-ups. Or maybe we both just lost count.

Either way, when I finished and stood, he threw a length of rope at me—except I now knew in the navy you called it a line and not a rope. He told me to tie that bowline I was so eager to tie.

I was too exhausted to be nervous; besides, I'd tied bowlines a thousand times since I was little and growing up around boats on Ocracoke Island, where every time you needed to tie just about anything to anything else you used a bowline, especially on a sailboat. My fingers were frozen, though, and I messed up twice, which surprised me. Chief rolled his eyes. Before he could say anything, though, I took a deep breath and I guess my hands had warmed up enough by then so I could feel what I was doing because my fingers sort of worked automatically to tie the knot. That time it took me about five seconds.

Chief snatched the line from me, inspected it, yanked on it, and cracked just the tiniest hint of a smile.

"You been around boats before, boot?" he asked. The other guys were straining to listen.

"Yes, Chief," I said. "Grew up on the Outer Banks in North Carolina."

"How old are you?"

"Seventeen, Chief," I said.

He shook his head. "How old are you really? Because I know they're taking anybody who can walk through the door on their own two feet, and half this company lied about their age to get here, and that baby face of yours has never even seen a razor before."

"Seventeen, Chief," I said again, my voice still shaking. "Honest."

He stared at me for a minute. Then he said, "All right, boot. I'll make a deal with you. Tomorrow, the company that has the highest success rate in knot tying wins the Rooster Flag. You seen the Rooster Flag?"

I nodded. We'd all seen it—a flag in the mess hall with a red rooster on a white background.

"The Rooster Flag goes to the top company of the day, and B Company here—Baby Company—is going to be just that for at least one day during boot camp. I want that one day to be this week, and to help me out with that you're going to teach every one of the men in this company how to tie a bowline—*and* a figure-eight, *and* a reef knot, *and* a clove hitch—by first light tomorrow. You do that and I'll put you in for whatever assignment you want once you graduate from boot camp. But if you don't, I'm finding out how old you really are, and then I'm sending you home to your mama so she can give you a good spanking for running away."

My heart sank. There was no way I could teach a hundred guys how to tie all those knots, no matter how many times I'd tied them myself.

"Company fall out!" Chief ordered. "Our littlest boot here is going to give you all a lesson in knot tying."

He pointed to a couple of wooden boxes that we'd been marching past since we'd been out on the Grinder. "You'll find all the line you need in there. Have at it."

I squeezed my eyes shut, wishing this could all disappear, or I could go back in time and not be so dumb as to raise my hand like some stupid little schoolboy. It was going to be a very, very long night.

CHAPTER 6

At first everybody crowded around me in a circle, and I was so nervous I couldn't speak. I fumbled with my line, and when I opened my mouth no words came out.

"Well, get on with it," a guy named Tony Spinelli barked. He had a New Jersey accent. I just hoped he didn't have a New Jersey temper, too.

"Okay," I finally managed to squeak. I held my line up in front of me, made a small loop, and then demonstrated. "You take this end and run it through here and around here and back through here and then you pull here and—"

"Can't hear you!" somebody said.

"Speak up!" somebody else added. "We'll be here all night if you don't speak up!"

I tried again but still couldn't seem to make myself heard over the guys stamping their feet on the frozen ground to keep the feeling in their toes. Plus I kept stuttering.

"What the heck's wrong with him?" Spinelli yelled. "I can't hear nothing! Chief's gonna make us stand out here forever waiting on this idiot."

"Hey," a familiar voice responded. "Don't call him that. He's doing the best he can. Just give him a second."

It was the big guy from before, who had grabbed my arm and told me he wouldn't want to see me trampled. The one who'd called me a boy and who I'd scowled at—and who'd laughed at me.

He stepped up beside me and put his hand on my shoulder. "It's okay, little buddy. I saw you tie that knot a minute ago. All you got to do is take it easy and explain it to the rest of us."

He held up his line to show me he was ready. Woody sort of inched up closer to us as well. He didn't say anything, but I appreciated that he was willing to stand by me, or at least kind of near.

"Go on, then," the big guy said. "You can do it."

I didn't know why he was being so nice to me, but I appreciated it so much that I took his line and quickly tied a bowline for him.

"There," I said. "Like that."

"Okay," the big guy said, taking back his line and studying the knot. "Only now you have to explain it so we can all do it."

I glanced up at him and nodded, then looked nervously around. A couple of guys were attempting with their lines but already looked hopeless trying to follow along. One of them threw his on the ground and stomped on it. Spinelli scowled at me—a real scowl, not like the one that didn't work when I tried to do it. His made me even more nervous.

But the big guy tapped me on the shoulder and that brought me back to what I was supposed to be doing.

"Maybe if you teach it to us the way it got taught to you, that'd be the way to do it," he said.

And I realized that was the answer. Dad had this special way of teaching the bowline, and I remembered it as clear as anything. It had worked for me when I was three years old, so it ought to work with grown men—or nearly grown men anyway.

"Okay," I said, starting over with my small loop and fighting to make my voice louder—and not stutter. "This is the bunny's hole."

Everybody started laughing. "Are you freaking kidding me?" Spinelli howled. "A bunny hole?"

The big guy turned to Spinelli and told him to just keep quiet and let me finish. Spinelli actually growled at him.

"I guess you could just call it a rabbit hole instead," I said.

"How about a hare?" somebody drawled in a thick Southern accent. "Ain't that another name for a bunny, too?"

"Hare today, gone tomorrow," somebody else chimed in. Everybody groaned when he said that.

"Anyway," I said, actually gaining a little confidence now that I'd started. "Bunny hole, rabbit hole, doesn't matter what you call it. This short end of your line is the bunny, and you start off holding it behind the hole. So what you do after that is your bunny comes out of the hole, goes around the tree, then goes back in the hole. Pull it tight and there's your bowline."

The guys laughed some more, and then they made me tell it to them again—and show them again.

"One more time," said Spinelli, who didn't sound mad anymore. At least he wasn't growling.

"Okay," I said, and I went through the bunny story a third time, and then they all tried it. Half got it on the first try, and just about the whole other half got it on the second. I couldn't believe it! Woody was the last to get it, but finally even he did as well, with those two guys punching on his arms the whole time.

The big guy patted me on the back—so hard he nearly knocked me down. "I knew you could do it," he said, reaching out to shake my hand.

Woody was standing right next to me now, too. "I knew you could do it, Danny," he said.

"Thanks," I sort of mumbled, even though I doubted that was true.

The big guy introduced himself—he said his name was Josef Straub—and I told him who I was, and who Woody was, and he said, "Well, nice to meet you, Danny. Now how about those other knots, 'cause it's getting mighty cold out here and there's a bunch more to go. More bunny holes and such you can tell us about?"

"No bunny holes," I said. "But there are some other tricks my dad taught me."

"Let's hear 'em, then," he said, and so we got back to work.

Once they had the bowline down, it didn't take very long at all for me to teach them the other knots Chief wanted us to learn, using Dad's knot stories from when I was little—even Woody, with his problem knowing his right from his left, figured it out. And once we showed Chief we'd mastered them, he let all the guys head over to the mess hall to be first in line for evening chow.

He held me back, though.

"I'm not in the habit of giving out compliments, boot," he said. "And if you tell anybody what I'm about to say, I'll deny saying it and you'll be out here doing drills by yourself on the Grinder all night long, understood?"

I nodded. "Understood, Chief." I wasn't stuttering, but my voice was back to being kind of shaky.

"All right, then," he said. "I don't know how old you are or you aren't, and quite frankly I don't care. I wouldn't bet on you being a day over fourteen, but, again, I don't care. The navy needs men. The war needs men. And those men need to know how to tie proper knots and at least a hundred of them now do thanks to you. So, good job."

"Thank you, Chief," I said.

"So what'll it be?" he asked.

I was confused. "What do you mean, Chief?"

"I told you if you could teach those numbskulls how to tie knots you'd get your pick of assignments. We have five more weeks of boot camp, but no reason not to say now. So what'll it be? Desk job? Signal corps?"

"Subchaser," I said, without even hesitating, the shakiness gone. "I want to be a subchaser."

Chief studied my face for a minute, as if he was looking for a clue to something. Then he said, "How come a subchaser?"

I couldn't tell him, but he guessed, of course.

"U-boat got somebody you know?"

I nodded.

"Somebody in your family, over there off the Outer Banks?"

I nodded again and felt the tears welling up behind my eyes. I couldn't speak or I knew I'd start crying, thinking about Danny, and I didn't want Chief to ever see me doing that.

He looked around, saw that there wasn't anybody else out on the Grinder—except Straub and Woody, who were waiting for me about twenty yards away in the direction of the mess hall—and put his hand on my shoulder. "I'll see what I can do to make it happen," he said, and then he dismissed me to go to the mess hall.

I noticed he stayed out on the Grinder by himself for a pretty long time, and it made me wonder if maybe a U-boat hadn't gotten somebody he knew, too.

If I thought Chief was going to go easy on me after that—or on the company—boy, was I ever wrong. A couple of nights later he woke us up again, banging on a trash can lid and yelling at us to "Move it, move it, move it!"

It was Spinelli's turn to be stupid. "But it's three o'clock in the morning. Do we have to?"

He was still in his skivvies when he said it, and that was as far as he got getting dressed because Chief blasted him: "It's not your mommy asking you! It's me and I'm telling you! And now you get fifty push-ups first."

So as the rest of us pulled on our uniforms and peacoats, there was poor Spinelli in his underwear struggling through his push-ups—and with Chief's boot on his rear end, too. I almost felt sorry for him, but mostly I was just glad it wasn't me again.

But then I remembered how much I appreciated Straub and Woody standing up for me, or with me, when I was trying to teach everybody to tie the knots, and decided I would hang back and wait for Spinelli—even though he was the guy giving me the hardest time about the knots.

"Those push-ups ought to be illegal so early in the morning," I said to him once he'd gotten dressed and we hustled to catch up to the rest of the company, which had already left the barracks.

"Ah, I can handle it," Spinelli said. "Ain't nobody soft that's from Jersey."

"Sure," I said. "But still lousy when it's you that's having to do them."

"You're right about that," he said. "Teach me not to open my big, fat mouth."

I laughed and he did, too, then we picked up the pace to catch up with the others.

"Hey, thanks for waiting for me," Spinelli said.

"I just wish we'd had time to go to the head," I said.

Spinelli suggested I try peeing while running, but I didn't think that was such a good idea. Maybe it was something they did in New Jersey. I made a note to ask him about it later on when I wasn't so out of breath.

CHAPTER 7

Five minutes later, Spinelli and I were past the Grinder down by the lake with the rest of the company, lifting these heavy whaleboats over our shoulders, thirteen of us to a boat, and jogging with them down to the shore. I could barely keep my hands on our boat since the other guys were holding it pretty high, so I knew I wasn't carrying my share of the load.

Once we were there I jumped in and grabbed an oar, but Chief had other ideas. He went from boat to boat tagging the smallest guy in each to be the coxswain—the guy who sits in the stern and yells out directions to the rest of the crew, which, of course, are all the guys pulling on the oars.

At first I felt bad that I wasn't doing my part, but then, because I wasn't exercising and the others guys were, they heated up and I just sat there and froze.

We spent the next freezing couple of hours rowing out onto the lake under a full moon, keeping the shoreline in sight as best we could, though most of the boats did a lot of zigging and zagging, the coxswains barking orders through their megaphones but having a hard time getting every-body's strokes coordinated. One boat was stuck going in circles. Several slammed into one another, and a couple threatened to capsize, which would have been murder to anybody who fell in, even with our life jackets on.

Somehow I managed to keep my crew working pretty much together and going in a straight line—or at least a straighter line than any of the others. It also helped that I was so skinny and we didn't have any extra weight in our whaleboat. Straub and Woody were on different boats. Spinelli was an oarsman on mine. He might not have been soft, coming from Jersey and all, but he was sweating a river and grunting with each pull on the oar just like everybody else on the boat—well, except for me.

Then Chief announced that we were going to race. He was standing at the end of the dock with a bullhorn when he told us. Then he pointed east, along the shoreline, and barked, "Go!"

Our boat jumped quickly into the lead, and pretty soon we started pulling away. I kept up the orders, having one side pull harder if we veered off course one way, and the other side pull harder if we went too far in the opposite direction. I kept the pace of the rowing steady, too. I'd been in enough rowboats to have some idea of what would work, even though I'd never done this coxswain thing before. My throat was raw from all the yelling, even with the megaphone, and after a while I started sweating, too, despite how cold and windy it was.

The only problem was I didn't know where we were racing to, and when I finally turned back to look, I couldn't see any of the other boats. I had the crew slow down until the other boats came into sight, but they never did. So we just waited, the waves rocking us and the night wind whistling through and making everybody chilled now that we were all sweaty but no longer working and no longer generating any body heat.

"We should have brought blankets," Spinelli grumbled.

"Do you guys think we should turn back?" I asked, but nobody said anything. They were just like me, though, I was pretty sure—gone from thinking we were the best boat on the water to wondering if we'd gotten lost, or hadn't heard an order, or something bad.

It turned out to be something bad, all right. When we returned to shore, Chief was furious at us for taking off the way we did and leaving the other boats behind.

"But you told us it was a race," Spinelli said, before the rest of us could stop him. "We thought we were supposed to go fast and win."

Chief turned red in the face and stepped over to confront Spinelli.

"And what happens if one of those other boats capsizes?" he demanded. "Who's gonna rescue those sailors who are in freezing water and drowning if you don't keep them in sight?"

"Uh, the other loser boats that are back there with them?" Spinelli answered.

Chief exploded. "Wrong! Race or no race, you are responsible for your fellow sailors. No man left behind."

Spinelli managed to keep his mouth shut after that, but the damage was done.

Chief didn't make us do push-ups. He made us carry all the whaleboats and oars back up to the boathouse and then clean and secure all the equipment while the rest of the company got to sit around a couple of fire pits and thaw themselves out and laugh at us. Then Chief ordered our crew to march over to the mess hall and peel potatoes.

I apologized to the other guys, but they all said I shouldn't worry about it. "It ain't your fault," Spinelli said as I scurried to keep up with the bigger guys holding a whaleboat over their heads so I'd at least be able to touch the side of the boat, even if I once again wasn't helping to actually carry it.

"Sometimes there just ain't no rules to follow," he continued, "except the ones in Chief's head that he decided not to share with the rest of us."

And that was how it went for the next five weeks at boot camp. More middle-of-the-night orders to "Move it, move it, move it!" and not knowing where we were supposed to be moving it to until we got there. More drilling on the Grinder. More seamanship classes. More calisthenics. More marksmanship training and heavy weapons training. More swimming and lifesaving and firefighting drills with protective suits and high-pressure water guns.

And more hanging out with Straub and Woody and Spinelli—sitting together at mess hall, trying to get assignments together. We kept an eye out for one another and made sure we were nearby to help each other out of any jams. Sometimes, though, we all managed to get in trouble together.

There was a mock ship inside an enormous warehouse they used to teach guys which way was forward and which way was aft, what was starboard and what was port, the difference between a forecastle and a pilot house and a flying bridge and all the other parts of a ship. We got there early for the class, so the other guys and I started goofing around, pretending we were playing war on this pretend ship, making explosion noises and machine-gun sounds and just generally acting like little kids.

But then the instructor showed up. At first he just glared at us. Then he told us we were being idiots, and did we have any idea what could actually happen to us if we weren't vigilant when we were out on patrol?

He rolled up his sleeve and showed us his arm—or what was left of his arm. It looked like red, raw hamburger meat. We could almost see the tendons underneath the thin flesh covering his elbow. He was missing three fingers.

"That's what a third-degree burn looks like," he said. "After it's healed. And after skin grafts and four surgeries."

We all got really quiet.

"It's from not being vigilant," he said, his voice getting louder. "It's from thinking this is all a big game and then all of a sudden there's an explosion and an oil fire on your destroyer. So that's when you find out it's not a game. Not to you, and especially not to your best friend, whose whole body and face looks like this arm."

He rolled his sleeve back down. And we stopped horsing around.

They gave us aptitude tests to see which jobs we were best suited for in the navy, and even though Chief had already promised me assignment to a subchaser, I had to take the tests like everybody else because they needed to know what I would actually be doing on the subchaser.

Most subchasers were this new class of smaller ships called patrol crafts that used underwater explosives like depth charges to damage or destroy U-boats—if they could catch them, which so far they hadn't had much luck doing. *Patrol craft* sounded like something you'd see tourists on for sightseeing around the Outer Banks in the summers. Before the war anyway.

Straub said he wanted to shoot big guns, and he didn't care what kind of boat he did it on. Spinelli said he'd take a desk job, which surprised me since he was always talking about how tough everybody from Jersey was and everything. Woody said maybe he'd like to work on engines.

The navy took down the information but didn't make any promises.

On Sundays, Chief made us all go to church, which was nice because it was the one time during the whole week when we got to just sit and do nothing. About the only rule Chief had for us in church was that we had to stay awake, which wasn't a problem for me with all the praying I was doing. But it was hard for a lot of the guys because of how tired we were and how hot it got in there with so many of us crammed together in the pews. Anybody Chief saw nodding off he made swab the barracks deck in the afternoon instead of playing football on the Grinder or seeing visitors at the reception building.

I prayed for Danny to get better and come out of his coma and not have anything too terrible wrong with him. I prayed for Mama to not be worried about me. I prayed for Dad, who I still missed even though he passed away four years ago. That was usually when I got homesick, when I was praying for all of them, and thinking so much about home, and remembering that just a few weeks before I was like anybody else who was twelve, studying the Revolutionary War, doing sums, diagramming sentences, and playing ball. Now that seemed so far away and long ago that it was like it had all happened to a different person.

After church was visiting hours, and guys who had family close by enough got to see their moms and dads and brothers and sisters and aunts and uncles and cousins hauling in baskets and buckets and coolers full of food that ended up getting shared with the rest of us afterward. But while the visitors were there, those of us without any family just made do the best we could since everybody felt some kind of lonely during that time.

We played checkers a lot, and cards. Spinelli tried to teach us chess, but Woody couldn't follow it to save his life, and Straub thought it was stupid that the queen had all the power but the king couldn't do much of anything except move one space at a time until he got killed.

"I don't see why he can't move however he wants, and as far as he wants, and jump over anybody he wants," Straub said. "I mean, he's the *king*, all right?"

Spinelli finally just gave up.

When we got tired of games, we caught up on our newspaper reading, which was something I'd never done much of in my whole life, but I thought it would make me look older if I took it up now. But the news just made me so mad. How long it was taking the United States—*us!*—to send troops over to Europe to actually fight the Germans instead of just sending supplies to Great Britain and the USSR. I mean, that was important, too, but when were we going to go to real war with the Nazis?

And those poor merchant marines running supplies across the Atlantic were getting sunk by the hundreds by U-boats and Nazi warships and Luftwaffe planes.

Not to mention the Eastern Seaboard of the US, where more and more cargo ships and passenger ships were being targeted by the U-boats to disrupt the supply lines back here at home, too.

I'd read about all that and a few times, without realizing what I was doing, I'd torn the newspaper in half, and then ripped it into smaller pieces, until Straub stopped me.

"Easy, little buddy," he said. "There's others who also want to read that."

I couldn't help it, though. I was always thinking about what happened to Danny and me that day, and then about Danny in the coma. It all just made me so mad I could spit.

So that was when my friends stepped in and dragged me away to play Ping-Pong, or shoot pool, or deal up some other card game—anything to take my mind off Danny, not that I'd told them what happened. But somehow they just seemed to know.

On payday I cashed my check at the bank on base. I was tempted to buy some clothes since I didn't have any except my uniforms but decided to send it all to Mama, the way I'd promised myself I would. Except for keeping enough to buy myself a candy bar, but that was all.

I wrapped the bills up good and tight and got a big envelope at the post office to mail it to Ocracoke Island. With a letter to Mama also tucked inside.

> *Dear Mama,*
> *I have been working like I told you but not in Morehead City. I can't tell you where, but I don't want you to worry. Everything is good. I have made some friends*

and we are always very busy and I've been staying out of trouble. Every Sunday I go to church and pray for you all.

I wanted to tell her everything that had happened since I left home. It didn't feel right to keep so much a secret from her. All my life, Mama had always known what I was up to. Living on an island, everybody knew everybody and you couldn't get away with anything without somebody telling your parents.

But I wasn't on the island anymore. So I made it a short letter and promised to write her again soon and send more money when I got my next paycheck. And signed it *Love, Colton.*

CHAPTER 8

A lot of guys' families came for graduation day from boot camp, but not mine or Woody's or Spinelli's. Straub's mom and dad came, though—they lived in Ohio so it wasn't too far for them to drive—and they adopted the rest of us for the afternoon. For once we got to sit at the long tables in the visitor center with baskets and coolers of decent drinks and chow, instead of having to wait for somebody's leftovers on visiting day.

Mr. and Mrs. Straub were both as big as their son, and it turned out that they were originally from Germany. Some people sitting nearby kept glancing over suspiciously when they heard the Straubs' accents, which maybe was partly why the Straubs weren't shy about telling us in their loud, booming German voices how much they hated Hitler, as if anybody might've had any doubts.

"What they say about him," Mrs. Straub said, "he is nothing but a bully all his life. Only he has his brown shirts—they do his bullying for him. And now his Nazis. He is a poison on the earth."

Mr. Straub agreed. He listed all the countries in Europe that Hitler had conquered, in order—a list Mrs. Straub punctuated by saying *"Mein Gott!"* after each one: Austria, Czechoslovakia, Poland, Denmark, Norway, Luxembourg, the Netherlands, Belgium, France, Yugoslavia, Greece. But when he finished, he said, "But not Great Britain! And not America!"

Then he changed the subject, encouraging us to eat more of these sausages he called bratworst, and this funny thing they did to cabbage that he called sauerkraut, and this heavy, sweet dessert called strudel. We got so stuffed that when Mrs. Straub launched into her I Hate Hitler rant again, all I could do was sit there and not move except to nod my head and then finally just doze off in my chair.

Later that afternoon, after my nap, the navy had us do some marching drills on the Grinder, with all the officers and some politicians sitting on a reviewing stand for us to salute as we went past. The families huddled in the cold March wind off to the side and applauded and cheered, which made us feel like we were real navy now, ready to go off and fight the Germans and the Japanese and be heroes.

When it was over and Chief dismissed us for the last time, he said, "Men, I know I've been hard on you from day one, and some of you hate me for it. As true as that may be, there will come a time when you will thank me, because as hard as you think it's been here in boot camp, it will be a hundred times harder out there. Harder to survive the boredom of days and days at sea with nothing happening. Harder to survive conditions on the ocean so terrible you won't think your ship—or you—can possibly survive. Harder to keep your wits about you when bombs are going off all around you, or hitting your ship. Harder to watch your shipmate perish right in front of your eyes—and know that you can't do anything for him and that you have to keep your head on your job and in the fight.

"The navy has prepared you the best we can up to this point. Your job from here on out is simple: to protect the United States of America, defeat Germany and Japan, and save the world."

He paused, then saluted and said, "Dismissed."

I went up to him afterward. "I, uh, just wanted to thank you, Chief," I mumbled, still a little scared of him.

He looked at me for a long time before he spoke.

"Son," he said. "It's not too late to go home. I know I should have said something before. There's a lot of pressure to recruit and train as many men as we can, as fast as we can, for the war effort. But, truthfully, you don't belong here. You and I both know you're way too young for this."

I didn't know what to say, though he waited. In that moment I wanted to go home. I knew I wasn't ready for whatever was coming next—which would take me even closer to the war, closer to getting shot at by U-boats, and farther away from my family.

I clenched my jaw. I wasn't going to quit, though. I just wasn't. I couldn't let Danny and Mama down. And with my teeth still clenched, I told him that.

Chief took off his hat and scratched his scalp. Then he shook his head. "Just don't go get yourself killed," he said. "Or if you do, make sure you take a whole lot of those Germans down with you."

CHAPTER 9

Two days later, Woody and me—now both seamen second class—were on a train for Miami, of all places, to the new Subchaser Training Center they'd just opened down there. It was the end of March, still winter on Lake Michigan, so we were ready to be in the tropics.

Chief had come through on my request for Woody to go with me, even though I wasn't sure why I had been asking except that Woody had begged me to.

"He's your headache now," Chief had told me, shaking his head. "In a better navy he'd have already been tossed out on his butt."

"I'm sure he'll do all right, Chief," I'd replied, though I wasn't at all sure. But like Chief said, Woody was my headache now. Once boot camp was behind us and we were rolling south on the train, he turned back into the Woody he'd been before, when I first met him on the bus five weeks earlier—talking nonstop about anything and everything back home in Kinston. I pulled my sailor cap down over my face, closed my eyes, and quit listening. Eventually, he must have run out of things to say, or maybe he fell asleep, too— probably in the middle of a sentence.

Straub was off for artillery training at a school on the West Coast. Spinelli had gotten his request for a desk job and was shipping out for New York—so basically he was going home, or close to it. We all said we'd keep in touch. I didn't know about them, but I meant it. I couldn't imagine how I'd have gotten through basic training without them. Even Woody.

I fell asleep on the long train ride down to Miami, and when I did I dreamed about me and Danny. Not the day of the U-boat, but another day, not long after Dad died, when we went riding on our beach ponies, splashing in and out of the surf, kicking up so much sand it felt like rain falling, only the sun was full and hot and bright overhead and everything looked silver. In my dream we were still riding and Danny was still beside me on his pony and we weren't sad about Dad because his dying wasn't real, and it seemed like we could go on like that forever—two kids running wild and free on Ocracoke Island.

It got hotter and hotter the farther south we went, and by the time we got to Miami, it was hard to remember how cold it had been in Illinois just two days before. We wouldn't be wearing our peacoats down here, that was for sure.

A navy truck took us to our quarters, and we couldn't believe it when we got there. It was this famous, giant hotel on Biscayne Boulevard called the Everglades, only they had emptied the tourists out of it so they could house all of us sailors and officers coming into town for subchaser school.

"I ain't never seen anything this big or this fancy," Woody marveled. I was thinking the same thing but didn't want to say it out loud.

All the fanciness ended inside, though. They had pulled up carpet and taken pictures and anything else of any value off the walls, so the Everglades was just a stripped-down version of what it used to be. Woody and I shared a room that had cots instead of beds, but we didn't mind, because at least we didn't have to sleep in hard bunks the way we had at Great Lakes.

The mess hall was in the Everglades dining room, which was enormous, but like the rest of the hotel no longer anything fancy. Same old navy chow. Cooks threw big portions of everything on our trays, all pretty much running together, and if there was dessert, they plopped that down on top of the meat and potatoes and peas. Ice cream started melting right away so we had to eat that first, of course.

"I don't know why I never thought of doing it this way all along," Woody said, ice cream dribbling down his chin until I shoved a napkin at him. "Don't save the best for last. Save it for first."

"Then you wouldn't exactly be saving it," I said.

Woody just shrugged. Then he insisted that we toast our first meal in Miami by clinking spoons full of melted ice cream.

The commanding officer of the Subchaser Training Center was Lieutenant Commander Eugene McDaniel. They herded all of us into a giant room at the training center after dinner for what was supposed to be orientation but was, instead, just him—a small, skinny guy with thinning hair and wire-rimmed glasses. He looked really mad, and it turned out he was.

"I do not want to be here," he began. "I want to be absolutely clear about that. I am only here because I was so ordered. I would rather be at sea fighting those Nazi beasts. Make no mistake about it. They must be hunted down and they must be destroyed. You will be the ones to do that, and if you're not committed to the cause, then I want you transferred out of this command immediately. When I came here the navy sent me six officers. I sent three of them back because they did not have sufficient training, experience, or, frankly, the guts and determination to get the job done. You may have heard that a civilian merchant unloaded his produce on a navy pier, and that I had it tossed. That story is true. That was my dock, strictly to be used for training. There's a war going on, and I do not have time or patience for anybody or anything that gets in the way of our winning it."

A guy elbowed me in the ribs. "Sounds like it's true, what they say about him."

"What's that?" I asked.

"Looks like a professor but fights like a pirate."

Lieutenant Commander McDaniel continued, his voice getting even sharper. "I have seen the fury of the Nazi submarine onslaught from firsthand encounters with their

U-boats. They are highly trained, they are stealthy, and they are murderous. They are going after our cargo ships and fully intend to cripple our war effort. Without supplies, our allies cannot defend themselves. Without the weapons we supply, without the oil and food and other material support we ship to them, the war against the Nazis will be lost. Without supplies for ourselves, we cannot defeat anybody.

"Right now, the Nazis are winning. If their rate of success sinking our supply ships in the North Atlantic continues, by this summer we will have lost hundreds of ships and thousands of men aboard those ships. These are men who are risking, and losing, their lives for the Allied cause. We will not allow this to continue. You will take the training you receive here and you will then take the fight to the Nazis— and you and I will defeat them."

He paused, took off his glasses, wiped them with a handkerchief, then put them back on.

"As you leave here today, I want you to look at something I have had placed right outside—so you can see it every day of your training. It is, or was, a lifeboat. Two months ago a navy destroyer went to the aid of a British cargo ship that had been hit by torpedoes. I was on that destroyer. By the time we arrived, the ship was sinking, so we began the search for survivors. Lookouts spotted a lifeboat—the life-boat you will see outside this room. No one on it was alive. It was riddled with bullet holes, splattered with blood, and littered with dead sailors."

He paused again. He picked up a glass of water and drank some. Then continued.

"What that meant, gentlemen, in case you are unfamiliar with how the Nazi beasts operate, is that after torpedoing the British ship, the U-boat surfaced, approached the lifeboat, and instead of taking prisoners as is required under international law, they uncovered their deck guns and machine-gunned those helpless, defenseless merchant sailors.

"We gave those sailors a proper burial at sea. I ordered their lifeboat lifted onto the ship and had it placed on the training grounds—bullet holes, blood stains, and all—as a constant visual reminder of why you are here."

And with that, Lieutenant Commander McDaniel turned and walked off the stage.

"Old Blood and Guts," the guy sitting next to me said. "That's what they call him. And I can see why."

I nodded, and so did Woody, sitting next to me on the other side.

We saw the bloody lifeboat when we filed out. It was sitting in the sand under a couple of low palm trees. All the bullet holes were marked with rings of white paint—and there were a lot of them, too many to count. There were dark stains inside the boat, soaked into the wood. I felt a chill just looking at it, even though it was sunny out and a hot eighty degrees.

CHAPTER 10

For the next six weeks we were even busier than we'd been in boot camp, learning everything Lieutenant Commander McDaniel ordered us to learn about protecting cargo ships and sinking submarines. A lot of it was what they'd already drilled us on over and over in boot camp, only now we knew it even better: seamanship, boat handling, damage control, firefighting, ship-to-ship communications. And a lot of it was figuring out how to spot a U-boat—the reflection off a periscope lens, a swell like the one that came up under Danny and me, a shadow just under the surface of the ocean—and how to tell the difference between a U-boat and something else, like a whale or a school of dolphins.

The first thing they taught us, though, was why the German submarines were called U-boats.

"Anybody know?" an instructor asked. There were at least a hundred of us crammed in a classroom made for maybe thirty.

A guy who didn't look much older than me raised his hand. I held my breath, wondering if it was going to be like boot camp, where a question wasn't really a question, and the instructor would yell at that kid and order him to do push-ups, or worse.

But the instructor just nodded at him and said, "Yes?"

"*Unterseeboot,*" the guy said.

A bunch of guys laughed. "Speak English!" somebody shouted.

The instructor told everybody to quiet down. "That's right," he said. "*Unterseeboot.* It's German. And do you know what it means, son?"

The kid looked like he wished he could disappear, but he answered, "Yes, sir. It just means 'undersea boat.' *Boot* is German for 'boat.'"

Somebody in the back of the room yelled out, "I'd like to take an *Unterseeboot* and kick Hitler in the butt with it," and everybody laughed again.

Much to the relief of the kid who was translating, the instructor moved on.

More classes followed that one. They taught us all about depth charges, which were big metal drums full of explosives that could be set to detonate at different depths, and how to launch them off our ships with what they called K- and Y-guns. They taught us how to shoot rocket bombs with devices called Hedgehogs. They taught us about how those depth charges and rocket bombs would also damage our own ships, and how we were supposed to do emergency repair when it happened—and when we got hit by somebody else's bombs, whether sub or ship or attacking plane.

Classes were mostly in sweltering Quonset huts, where everybody sweated through their clothes in the Miami heat and stunk up the place. When they lit up cigarettes in there, too, I thought I would pass out. A lot of guys smoked cigarettes, or used chewing tobacco or dip. Woody said he'd done it all, growing up in tobacco country, but I never saw him with a cigarette, tin, or pouch, and he actually turned green during an especially smoky class one day and went outside and threw up.

I stayed away from all that tobacco because I knew Mama wouldn't want me to ever do any of that stuff.

On Saturday we went out to sea on our first practice run on a patrol craft, which was about 170 feet long and had a crew of sixty men and five officers. The PC's job was to escort cargo ships and troop transports and protect them from U-boats. The commanding officer was a lieutenant named Chris Foss, and he introduced us to the ship while we were still tied up to the dock.

"Think of it as a sort of mini-destroyer," he said when we all gathered on deck. Woody and I had been assigned to the same ship, and as usual he was standing right next to me like he thought we were under orders to literally stick close together.

"These PCs were designed for one single purpose, and that's antisubmarine warfare," Lieutenant Foss said. He was above us on the bridge. "Most of you will be assigned to a PC once you finish your training, so no better time than the present to learn everything there is to know." He tapped the rail. "This baby can trail a U-boat at its maximum speed, and it's got the navy's best sound equipment. A PC is more maneuverable than a sub, and it presents a small target for a sub to evaluate, so there's less chance of a PC catching a torpedo, which should mean a greater chance of a PC catching the sub."

Woody elbowed me. "Sounds like he's trying to sell us a car," he whispered.

A petty officer was standing behind us. He leaned close to Woody's ear and hissed, "I'll be having words with you later, sailor. Now shut it while the captain is talking."

I thought Woody was going to faint. I inched away from him, wishing I'd been standing next to somebody else.

Lieutenant Foss was explaining all about the PC's two diesel engines, how seaworthy it was, and how it was possible to practically spin it on an axis near the mast. He said the ship was designed so that in rough seas it could right itself even if it rolled 110 degrees, which would mean the ship could be almost upside down and still not capsize. That was kind of hard to believe. I'd been on a lot of boats, and in some very big waves, but I'd never seen anything like that.

Then he stopped for a minute, maybe to let us absorb all the information he was giving us about the patrol craft, or maybe to change the subject.

"You will hear people—good navy people—refer to the patrol craft fleet, and all of you who will serve on a PC, as the Donald Duck Navy. Small ship, thin hull, limited fire-power. But what you will be doing is no joking matter. And how well you are trained to do it is something your instructors are dead serious about. Dead serious because if you don't learn everything about antisubmarine warfare stone cold—eat it, sleep it, breathe it—you and the ships and the people you are sworn to protect will end up at the bottom of the ocean."

He paused again while we all looked at one another, wondering what he was going to say next.

"U-boats are not true submarines," he continued. "They are warships that spend most of their time on the surface. Their deck-mounted guns are more powerful than yours will be. They can submerge for limited periods, but they can do a lot while they're there. They can travel anywhere from sixty to a hundred miles underwater at a time—to attack our ships, evade our pursuit, and escape the bad weather that will neutralize your effectiveness, but not theirs.

"A U-boat crew can clear its bridge, close hatches, and dive to periscope depth in thirty seconds. Half a minute and they're ready to fire a twenty-foot-long torpedo at you or at one of the ships you are sworn to protect. That means after a U-boat sighting, you have even less time than that to get to general quarters. In order to attack that submarine when you see it submerge—instead of just dodging its torpedo, or worse, watching helplessly as it sinks another ship in your convoy—you must be able to scramble to general quarters in twenty-five seconds.

"You will begin training to do this"—he paused to set his stopwatch—"RIGHT NOW!"

And at that, a Klaxon horn sounded the call to general quarters. We'd all been assigned a post already—mine was loading 34-pound shells into the 3"/50-caliber gun just below the bridge; Woody's was in the engine room—so we all took off and immediately started running into one another, knocking each other down, blocking somebody else's way. Guys were screaming at one another so loud that nobody could hear anything. The officers roared at us and shoved guys this way and that way, but we couldn't seem to get anywhere. And I was only trying to make my way about ten feet from where I started!

Maybe it was because I was so small, but the jostling forced me closer and closer to the edge of the ship until I was clinging to the rail to keep from going over the side—and then, next thing I knew, a couple of big guys slammed into me and I lost my grip and over I went, twenty feet down and straight into the water.

I'm not sure anybody even noticed. No horns sounded, no whistles blew—I knew that much. I found my sailor's cap and stuffed it in my pocket and swam over to the dock, though it was hard going in my work shirt and dungarees and boots. By the time I hauled myself out and walked the gangplank back onto the patrol craft, everybody had miraculously found their way to wherever they were supposed to go—except me. My boots made a squishy sound as I navigated over to the deck cannon and the pile of shells I was supposed to help load for us to fire at whatever U-boat might have been on the attack.

Lieutenant Foss glared at me from the bridge, as if he thought I'd deliberately jumped in to go swimming. I felt guilty even though I knew it wasn't my fault, but there was no way to explain.

"Five minutes," he said. "That took five minutes. Congratulations. You're all dead."

I found out later that Woody didn't do much better down in the engine room, two decks below and as far aft as you could go on the ship. Twelve guys packed in there like sardines at first, only as soon as Woody got there the engine room chief ordered eight of them to turn around and make their way back topside to load depth charges. He gave Woody some kind of order that Woody couldn't remember when he told me about it, because when the chief said "port side" he went starboard instead, hit his head on a pipe, and knocked himself out.

The next day was a Sunday, but instead of going to chapel, Woody went off somewhere by himself. He didn't tell me where, but I didn't mind having a few hours to myself. I went to chapel and prayed for Mama and Danny and everybody else on Ocracoke. The minister had us all pray for our troops and ships fighting the Japanese out in the Pacific. And he had us pray for the poor Soviet people in Leningrad, which was surrounded by Hitler's army and under siege. It was threatening to fall like every other city in the Soviet Union had fallen to the Nazis. And finally, he had us pray for the British tank forces who were battling the German army under Field Marshal Rommel for control of North Africa—and not faring very well.

So far we'd been sending supplies and weapons and food to England and the Soviet Union under President Roosevelt's Lend-Lease Act, but people were still wondering when America and the Allies would be able to launch a counterattack against Germany and Italy, a full-on invasion to take back France and liberate the rest of the European countries that Hitler had steamrolled with his blitzkriegs. Right now,

England was the only holdout, besides the Soviets. And it didn't seem like either one of them could hold out for much longer without our help.

And meanwhile, the German U-boats kept sinking more and more of our cargo supply ships all along the East Coast and down in the Caribbean and the Gulf of Mexico.

I was lying on my bunk that afternoon thinking about all that, and missing Mama and Danny and home, when Woody came back from wherever he'd been. It didn't take long to get it out of him. He rolled up his sleeves and showed me: On his right forearm he'd gotten a tattoo that said *Starboard* and on his left arm he had one that said *Port*.

"Should have done this a long time ago," he said, rubbing the bruise on his forehead where he'd run into the pipe. "Now that I know which direction is which, I'm ready to go hunt us down some U-boats."

CHAPTER 11

My next paycheck I also cashed and mailed to Mama, along with another letter telling her I was good and that I was praying for Danny and for all of them. It was probably word for word about the same letter as I'd written before from Great Lakes, but I couldn't really tell her anything else, so I figured the same was better than nothing.

The day I got the check was my thirteenth birthday, so at least I wasn't as underage as I used to be. I kept a dollar out of my paycheck to treat myself to a burger and a Coke at the commissary, which was a kind of general store they had on base, and another dollar so I could treat Woody, too, since he was the closest I had to a best friend in the navy. He kept pestering me about why I was being so generous and what was the big occasion?

"I ain't never seen you spend even a nickel before," he said as we walked over to the commissary. It was another Sunday. We only had two weeks left at the Subchaser Training Center, two weeks left in Miami.

"Heck, I don't even have a nickel left out of my paychecks," he added.

I shrugged. "I send mine home. They need it a lot more than I do."

"Yeah, guess I ought to be doing that, too," Woody said. "Only I ain't never got to have any money of my own my whole life. Even when I was cropping tobacco, my mom took it all from me. Said I owed it for rent."

"For rent?" I asked. That didn't make any sense. Nobody paid rent to stay in their own bedroom at their own house.

But apparently Woody did. "My dad left us when I was little, and we ain't seen him since. He wasn't good for nothing anyway. So my mom, seems like she always had one boyfriend or another around, and not much time for us kids. She was working and all, too. And she said we had to work if we were going to stay in the house. So that's what we did, from the time we couldn't hardly even walk."

"Sorry," I said. "That sounds rough." I told him I'd lost my dad, too. "But he didn't leave us," I quickly added. "I mean, not on purpose."

"What happened?" It was Woody's turn to ask questions. We were almost at the commissary but stopped to finish the conversation.

"There was a storm, and he didn't make it back to the island in time. He'd been out fishing. They said the waves got to thirty feet. They never found the boat, or any of the men. But I knew in my heart that however it happened, Dad would have been the one doing everything he could to try to save the others."

I paused for a minute because I was getting kind of choked up, then I swallowed hard and told Woody the rest of the story—how after the official search ended, Mama wouldn't give up, and day after day for probably two weeks she took me and Danny out in the skiff to look for any sign of Dad's boat. Nobody had the heart to tell her there was no point to it. Nobody on the island said much of anything except how sorry they were about Dad. It was like everybody had agreed to just pretend Mama wasn't doing what she was doing.

The way Danny had explained it to me was that Mama wasn't ready to let Dad go just yet, and us going out to search for him was her working up to the idea that he was gone forever, that he wasn't coming back, and that we were going to have to be a family without him.

Finally, the last day we went out, Mama had turned the boat around after just an hour. She didn't say anything at first, didn't speak at all until we made it back to the island and docked the boat.

Then she'd hugged Danny and me, sighed, and said, "I am sure going to miss him."

Danny had whispered, "Me too."

I hadn't said anything. I'd hated every second we were out on the ocean looking, but now that Mama had let us know she was done, I'd realized I wasn't ready to let go.

I was too little to take the boat out, so every day for a month I'd climbed the highest dune on the island with a pair of binoculars and searched for Dad that way.

Of course, he never did come back home.

Woody and I sat quietly for a while after I told him my story. We'd both been through a lot of sadness about our dads, and sometimes there just wasn't much to say.

I was the one who finally broke the silence.

"Anyway, it's my birthday today," I told Woody. "So we're celebrating."

"Whoa!" Woody exclaimed, happy to change the subject. "How old are you? Eighteen? That ain't possible, young as you look. You don't even shave yet."

He grabbed me around the neck and rubbed his knuckles hard on my scalp. With my navy buzz cut I didn't have any hair for protection, so it burned and I howled in pain.

"Happy birthday, Danny!" Woody shouted. And then, as we stepped into the commissary, he shouted to everybody who was there that it was my birthday and the next thing I knew they were all singing "Happy Birthday to You" like a bunch of kids at a party. Somebody even gave me a stale doughnut that must have been sitting around since early that morning and stuck a lit match in it for me to blow out like it was a candle.

It wasn't the best birthday I'd ever had, but it ended up not being too bad. Plus now I was officially a teenager.

In the last couple of weeks at subchaser school I spent hours in classrooms and on board learning how to operate sonar to locate U-boats underwater and enemy ships above it—while Woody got his crash course in operating, maintaining, and repairing patrol craft engines. They had a simulated ship interior in a warehouse, where they drilled us in fighting fires and shoring up bulkheads damaged by torpedo hits or by the concussive effects of our own depth charges. They trained us in lifeboat survival, and we spent hours rowing until we thought our arms would fall off—and still kept rowing for hours after that.

They tried having us learn cold water survival techniques, but the ocean was too warm, and they couldn't get the pool cold enough no matter how much ice they dumped in. We practiced firing machine guns from our patrol craft at targets towed behind old biplanes out over the ocean so we wouldn't hurt anybody, though a couple of guys aimed a little too close to the planes and that was the end of their target practice.

Woody always came back from his training covered head to toe in grease, which never seemed to come all the way off, no matter how hard he scrubbed in the shower and no matter how black the tile floor got. I got more and more sunburned from standing and staring through binoculars from the lookout post—what they called the crow's nest—on our patrol craft off Miami Beach, scanning the ocean for any sign of one of the US Navy submarines stationed out there for our training exercises. I looked like an owl with white circles around my eyes from having the binoculars pressed there for so long. So far I was the only one to spot a periscope, though it was in calm water, no waves to cut into visibility—besides, I knew it was out there somewhere.

"The biggest challenge you'll face, once you're deployed, won't be identifying the thing you're looking for, although that will be a huge challenge, too," Lieutenant Foss said. "But the biggest challenge will be boredom and fatigue. Hours and hours on your watch, watching and waiting. Your mind will wander. It's just human nature. But you can't let it be *your* human nature, because if you're not vigilant, people die."

It was the same with the sonar—training myself to pay attention the whole time I was on duty. I hadn't ever had much patience growing up. Danny was always the patient one. I was the one who jumped out of bed first thing in the morning and raced down to the beach to see what might have washed up overnight. And I was the one always getting guys to play baseball after school, or catch and tame the beach ponies, or have races during recess, or go body surfing. Mama said I must've been part dolphin, probably because of what a good swimmer I was and how much I liked to be in the ocean, and probably because I was always moving all the time.

But now I had to just sit there with the headphones on and listen for the pings of the sonar bouncing off objects underwater that I couldn't see, and learn to tell which ones were schools of fish, or sharks, or dolphins, or ocean junk, or boats skimming the surface, or coral reefs—or submarines—and how deep they were, how fast they were going, and what direction they were going. There was a lot of math involved in the calculations, too.

They told us sonar was invented by bats and dolphins, but what they meant was that bats and dolphins did it naturally to find their prey or whatever—send out these sound waves and then have them come back to them when the waves bounced off something. It was called echolocation, which sounded like a mouthful, but made sense once they explained. I doubted the bats and dolphins had to do the math part, though.

Once again a lot of guys' families came for graduation-day ceremonies, but none for Woody or me. Just before things got started, as we were walking over from our hotel to the subchaser school, we saw a couple of other sailors holding a newspaper and talking loudly about something in it.

"What's the news?" Woody asked.

One of the guys stabbed his finger into a picture on the front page of the paper. It was a plume of black smoke out in an otherwise cloudless April sky over the ocean. "Right off Jacksonville Beach," the guy said. "People out on the beach with their families, and right there a mile out, U-boats sunk a passenger ship, the USS *Gulfamerica*. Everybody saw it. Kids and everything. Couple of hours later, bodies washed up on shore."

"There's been a lot more ships sunk by U-boats than they're telling people about," his friend added. "On account of they don't want people to be too worried. But they couldn't keep this one quiet. Not when your kid's playing in the waves and up washes somebody dead."

"Murdered, you mean," said the other guy.

Suddenly, I was ready to skip the graduation and get my ship assignment right then and there—and give those Nazis what they deserved. "I want to track them down and sink every last one of them," I said fiercely.

The two friends nodded. "Course you better take us with you," one of them said. "Little fellow like yourself ain't going to be able to whip all those U-boats on your own."

Woody punched me on the arm. "He might be little, but he's a tough one, all right," he said. "Plus he's got eyes like an eagle. Can spot a U-boat just *thinking* about raising a periscope."

The two guys laughed. "Well, then, those Nazi U-boats—don't sound like they'll be around these parts much longer."

I just grinned and we all headed off for the graduation. I held on to the newspaper, though, and kept looking at that column of smoke rising out of the ocean off Jacksonville Beach, and thinking about those people who saw it—and, later, found the bodies washed up on shore. They would probably know a little bit about how I felt after the U-boat wrecked Danny's boat and put him in a coma—and how I would keep feeling until every last one of those *Unterseeboot*s was under the water for good.

CHAPTER 12

A week later, Woody and I were on the train again, heading to Michigan of all places—though not back to boot camp. Instead, we were going to Bay City, where a company called the Defoe Boat and Motor Works was building patrol crafts and had just finished the one we would be on, me as a sonar operator and signalman and Woody in the engine room as what they called a snipe, which was about the lowest-level engine room job there was.

The officers had already prepared our PC, so pretty much as soon as we got there—on a cold day in late spring—the sixty of us that made up the crew shouldered our sea bags and marched up the gangplank and on board for our shake-down cruise.

The chief petty officer, whose last name was Kerr and who didn't seem to have a first name, was a tall, wiry guy with a jaw that looked like it'd been chiseled out of stone. He was the one who greeted us—by barking orders at us to stow our gear first thing. He called us deck apes and said we'd better "Move it, move it, move it!" making me think he'd spent some time drilling recruits at boot camp. But there wasn't time to ask him—not that I was so dumb that I ever would, of course—as we made our way belowdecks to the crew's quarters in the forecastle, which was the forward part of the ship, just behind the head, and the worst place of all because that was where the ship would rise and fall the most in rough water.

We wedged our gear into lockers that were about half the size we needed, then made up our bunks, slipping fart sacks over mattresses, adding on folded blankets, and then doing what they called tricing up the bunks to the walls in the up position using chains at the foot and head of each bed. They said we had to do this to make more room in the narrow galley, but really it was to keep guys from sneaking naps on their bunks when they were supposed to be on duty.

Because I was the lowest-ranking seaman I got last pick of the bunks. Mine was as far forward as you could go in the crew's quarters, which I knew would make a bad situation even worse when I tried to sleep in the stormy ocean. Plus I'd get the stench from the head. Plus they made me take the top bunk—the third one up—which was almost higher than I could climb.

Before I could try to climb up on my own, though, somebody grabbed me from behind and without saying a word threw me onto the bunk. I slammed against the wall and yelped, and the rest of the crew laughed.

I heard a familiar laugh—deep and loud—and knew right away who it was.

"Straub!" I shouted. "What are you doing here?"

"They needed some muscle around those depth charges," he said. "And they figured I was the guy, even if I didn't get to go to your little submarine school."

I practically hugged him, and then said, "Want me to throw you up on your bunk next?"

Straub tipped his head back and roared. "I still don't know how you escaped from kindergarten and made it into the navy, but glad to see you, Danny."

That broke the ice with the other guys down there with us making up their bunks, and everybody started introducing themselves to everybody else. I couldn't believe I hadn't spotted Straub before when we were first coming on board the ship, as big as he was. I guess I'd just been too excited, and nervous, about getting my assignment and getting out on the Atlantic Ocean and going after those U-boats.

Woody, meanwhile, had followed the chief motor machinist's mate—another big guy, with red hair, who Woody later told me the other motor machinists and snipes called Big Carrot. All the engine crew slept where they worked, closer to the back of the ship in a compartment just off the engine room, so at least the rough water wouldn't be as much of a problem, even if the stink of twelve bodies crammed back there, coupled with the grease and fumes from the engine, made it hard to breathe—or to *want* to breathe!

Boy, was he ever surprised to see Straub when the snipes came back up on deck. They pounded on each other's backs so hard that they probably left big bruises.

That all stopped when Chief Kerr ordered us to stand at attention—adding at least a dozen cusswords to the order, which seemed to be just how he talked. Some of them actually made me turn red in the face to hear them. But I did what he said, just like everybody else.

We were waiting for Lieutenant Walter Talley to address the crew.

He kept us waiting for a really long time. Half hour. Forty-five minutes. An hour.

And then finally he showed, standing on the bridge, staring down on us, still at attention but not happy about it. We weren't supposed to look around, but it was hard not to check him out—what he looked like and all. He was young, maybe in his midtwenties, and clean-shaven, and must have just joined the navy right out of college—which turned out to be the case. Chief Kerr was what they called a navy lifer—he'd been in the service since the Great War—but Lieutenant Talley had just taken a bunch of officers' classes, along with training in antisubmarine warfare at the Subchaser Training Center. He was the one who would be captain of our ship, PC-450, which didn't have a name because they told us that in the Donald Duck Navy the ships were too small to deserve one.

Lieutenant Talley nodded a few times as if he were counting heads, then he took a deep breath in and seemed to hold it. I realized I was also holding my breath, and so were some of the guys around me. When Lieutenant Talley finally breathed out, we did, too. "Welcome aboard, men," he said in a stilted voice. "This is your new home. I can't tell you for how long. That depends on how long the war goes on. But anyway, welcome." He paused as if he was gathering himself for whatever else he had to say, but instead he just said, "Follow orders. Be where you're supposed to be at all times. Do your part to defeat the enemy. Take care of your fellow sailors. No exceptions." And then he said, "Dismissed."

Two weeks later, after our shakedown cruise on Lake Huron, it was time for our first mission—escorting a convoy of cargo ships out of New York Harbor. We got there on an evening in late May, all hands on deck to marvel at the spectacular city lit up. I could see everything: the Statue of Liberty and Ellis Island and the Empire State Building. All those famous places I'd heard about but didn't ever think I'd get to see.

"You think we'll get to go on shore?" Woody asked Straub and me, joining us to lean on the railing. I couldn't stop staring. "I bet there's all kinds of girls just waiting to go out on a date with a bunch of sailors like us," he added. "You know, navy heroes and everything."

Straub laughed his big laugh. "I don't remember us doing anything heroic just yet," he said.

"I ain't never seen so many lights in my whole life," Woody said, adding a whistle of amazement. "And you couldn't pay me enough money to go up in them tall buildings they got over there. I'd get scared of the heights just going up the stairs."

"They got elevators, you know," Straub said, as if he'd spent his life in a big city instead of some small town in Ohio.

"Same thing," Woody said.

Chief Kerr joined us then.

"Stupid idiots," he swore.

That caught me by surprise. "Sorry, Chief," I stammered. "We just haven't ever seen anything like this before."

"I'm not talking about you sailors," Chief said. "I'm talking about the stupid idiots who still won't order them to black out the lights in these cities at night. As if a dimout is enough. It's still a blazing bull's-eye. You don't think there's U-boats out there right now with the same view as us? Probably smiling away, sizing up targets. Ships coming in here, backlit by all those city lights. Heck, they could take out one or two of those buildings if they had a mind to."

I looked around nervously at the dark water surrounding us, kicking myself for not already having thought about what the chief said. This was the war, and here we were talking about riding in elevators in New York City and going on shore leave and girls.

"Back to your stations," Chief said. "You've seen your New York—or all of it you're gonna see this time around."

"Aye-aye, Chief," we said at the same time. It wasn't our watch yet, but we knew better than to say that, and instead we scattered to either hit our bunks and catch some shut-eye, or go down to the galley or somewhere else to hide. On the way I took a last look around, first inland at New York Harbor and the dangerous lights of the city, and then behind us where there was a fleet of cargo ships ready to begin their voyages, and beyond those were several navy destroyers and PCs that would be joining us when we set out for Key West in a couple of days.

I hoped they were being vigilant, the way that instructor had told us back on the pretend ship at basic training, the way we were also going to have to be vigilant from now on if we were going to protect the merchant ships on our convoy—and ourselves—from the U-boats lurking out there in the dark Atlantic, just waiting for an opportunity to sink us all.

CHAPTER 13

Our job was to escort supply ships from New York down to the Naval Air Station off the tip of Florida in Key West. We had to be on high alert for U-boats lurking around the shipping lanes along the East Coast—probably the same U-boats that had sunk ships near Ocracoke and in sight of all those people on Jacksonville Beach were still out there. Along with who knew how many others. There were three patrol crafts, including ours, protecting a dozen cargo ships loaded with weapons, food, vehicles, spare parts, and a hundred other things needed to keep a thousand-man naval base in operation.

Destroyers and planes from the Naval Air Station Key West had their own job to do—patrolling the Caribbean and the Gulf of Mexico in case Germany tried to sneak attack the US. Plus they had to keep the shipping lanes open for oil and other products we needed from South America going up to ports in Houston and New Orleans.

For the first couple of days, no matter whose watch it was, hardly anybody on our patrol craft slept. I knew I didn't. I couldn't say about Woody, because the engine crew kept pretty much to themselves, but from what he'd told me, their chief had Woody working himself stupid doing back-to-back watches.

I spent one watch in the sonar room and my next watch in the crow's nest on lookout duty, scanning the silver ocean for signs of U-boat activity until I thought I was going blind. But after those first few days of a whole lot of nothing—no pings on the sonar to indicate submarine activity, no telltale reflections off periscopes poking up out of the waves to take the measure of us and our convoy—it was impossible for our minds not to wander to other things, like how nasty all our uniforms were getting and how bad everybody smelled after all these sweaty days at sea.

The captain had given the order that nobody could take a shower. The plan was for the convoy to make the East Coast run without stopping at any of the ports along the way, so we had to preserve our supply of fresh water.

Not only that, but we could only brush our teeth twice a week. So everybody was getting pretty ripe. Then, to make matters even worse, the cooks served up beans for dinner two nights in a row, and all the fart sacks in the world wouldn't have been any help in containing the gas attack that hit us next.

Straub actually came crawling out through the canvas hatch onto the deck one evening, gagging from the smell and saying he felt like he was going to be sick. I didn't put too much stock in what he said, since he had such a weak stomach and got seasick any time the ocean got any kind of rough. But then I went below and the stench hit me like a baseball bat, and I turned right back around and crawled out behind him.

Finally, Chief Kerr took pity on us and told us to tie up all our dirty uniforms and toss the lines over the stern. The whole crew was in just skivvies and boots and sailor caps and that was about all while we washed our clothes like that, pulled along behind the ship for fifteen minutes until Chief ordered us to haul in the lines, and then he had us lay our clothes out all over the deck in the afternoon sun. They dried fast and smelled a lot better, but now everything was stiff and salt-encrusted, and chafed our sunburned skin when we put it all back on.

And there was still the problem of none of us having bathed in a week and stinking to high heaven, as Straub put it. But at least the cooks quit serving us beans.

The officers kept drilling us all the time, day and night, to make sure we were always prepared—and were able to be at general quarters in twenty-five seconds when we spotted a U-boat. So far, though, there'd still been a whole lot of nothing. The only excitement on the sonar turned out to be a school of dolphins. Two of the merchant ships miscalculated one of the zigzag turns and nearly rammed each other but were able to veer away at the last minute. A light rain turned a little heavier, and a few guys got seasick, but that passed pretty quickly, too.

And then one afternoon, halfway down the East Coast, a couple of miles off the North Carolina shore, I spotted something. I was up in the lookout post, trying not to think about how close we were to Mama and Danny, scanning all around with the binoculars, when a glint of light reflected off something silver and shiny out in the calm ocean. The convoy was plowing along at twelve knots—a little under fifteen miles an hour—fast for us, but the conditions were good. I didn't sound the alarm, because I didn't want to be the boy who cried wolf. I scanned back to where I'd just seen the reflection, but now I couldn't find it. I rubbed my eyes and then returned to the binoculars, sweeping back and forth over that quadrant of ocean. Still nothing.

And then, just when I was convinced my mind—or my eyes—had played a trick on me, I saw it again. A periscope!

I sounded the alarm and pointed so the officer of the deck on the bridge down below could see it, too, and the Klaxon blared the call to general quarters. Guys scrambled up from belowdecks to their battle stations, and the pilot swung us away from the convoy to give chase to the U-boat. Meanwhile, whoever was in the sonar room must have located it, too, because we had a more precise location and soon were at twenty knots and then more, racing toward the submarine!

I stayed at my post to try to find and maintain visual contact, while below me the guys were busy turning the guns, loading shells, and preparing to launch depth charges. My heart was pounding so hard I could practically hear it, and

I wished I had a weapon, even though there wasn't anything I could do with it from where I was. My weapon was the binoculars and helping locate the enemy.

And then we lost the contact. As hard as I tried, I couldn't see anything—no periscope, no nothing. Word came up from the sonar room that there were no pings, either, not even faint ones to indicate something large underwater moving away from us, like a U-boat retreating.

We searched the area for half an hour to be sure but still didn't turn up anything. Our signalman and our radio operator had alerted the merchant ships and the other escort vessels—two PCs, one flanking the convoy on the starboard side and the other trailing—but they couldn't find anything, either. I felt bad—and afraid Chief Kerr and Lieutenant Talley would think I *was* the boy who cried wolf, but that didn't happen. When my watch ended and I climbed down from the crow's nest, Chief told me I'd done a good job. "You saw it before sonar picked it up."

"But we didn't find anything, Chief," I said.

"Doesn't mean there wasn't something there," he responded. "For all you know, we saved a ship today, chased off a U-boat before it could get close enough or have time to aim and fire off a torpedo. Some things you just can't know.

But that doesn't mean you can ever relax, because even if there wasn't something there today—and I'm not convinced there wasn't—there *will* be something tomorrow, or the next day, or the day after that. And it wants to do one thing and one thing only, and that's sink this convoy."

CHAPTER 14

The next afternoon I was in the crow's nest on lookout again, only it was rougher seas, waves tall enough to hide a periscope half the time, though at least that meant a U-boat wouldn't be able to set its sights on any of our ships very well, either. But I still managed to spot another one before sonar picked it up—a periscope, no doubt about it, which meant a sub possibly preparing to launch torpedoes. I sounded the alarm and the call to general quarters went out, our PC lurching away from the convoy to give chase before the U-boat could fire. We made slower progress through the heavy waves, so we couldn't get there in time to fire our depth charges at the sub once it submerged.

We all held our breath and scanned the ocean for any sign of a torpedo just under the surface, blasting toward a hull riding low in the water under a full load of cargo. But there was nothing, so after a few minutes we could all exhale.

I kept up my search through the binoculars—not just in the direction of the U-boat that had disappeared on us, but farther afield as well. We all knew the U-boats traveled in what they called wolf packs, stalking convoys like ours, one U-boat running reconnaissance and the others somewhere ahead, setting a trap for whoever, or whatever, was coming. And sure enough, an hour later, there, ahead of the convoy, I spotted another periscope. Once again I gave the signal and out went the call to general quarters, only this time the captain gave the order for the battery team to aim the big 3"/50-caliber and fire. I was surprised by how quickly they did, and seconds later there was a terrific explosion and an enormous plume of water shot up into the sky.

"We got one!" I yelled, though there wasn't anybody near to hear me, especially with the engines racing below and the ship hammering through the waves. "We got one!"

Only it quickly became apparent that we hadn't got one. We hadn't gotten anything. So the order went out to fire again, and again, and as we drew closer, the captain also gave the order to launch depth charges. I guessed the sonar guys must have found our target by then and were able to home in on it quick.

When the depth charges detonated, it felt as if our PC was blown ten feet straight out of the ocean. I pitched wildly on the lookout platform and thought I was going to fall off—or be flung out—far over the deck and into the ocean. The next depth charge rocked us again. It was like riding a wild bronco the way the ship bounced and slammed hard back down. Alarms went off signaling men to go below for emergency repairs, which we'd drilled for a hundred times, the same as we'd done drills for general quarters and the rest.

I searched the ocean for signs that we'd actually hit the U-boat—an oil slick, pots and pans, mattresses, bodies—but nothing came up. The convoy steamed ahead, but we held back, circling the area where we'd dropped the depth charges and shelled with the forward gun.

Once again the U-boat had gotten lucky. But so had we.

Our luck didn't hold for too long, though. Over the next couple of hours those rough waves grew even rougher and more ominous as afternoon turned into evening. We caught back up to the convoy, at least for a while, but as the waves kept growing higher, pretty soon our attention turned fully to just trying to stay afloat. The storm would protect the convoy from any U-boat wolf pack, but for now, as we pressed on south through the black sea and sky, it was every ship for itself.

That wasn't a problem for the merchant ships, as big and heavy as they were, lumbering along, but it made things a lot more difficult for us PCs. We soon found ourselves climbing up the steep front of giant waves, then cresting at the top with the bow and what seemed like the whole front half of the ship out of the water, and then racing down the other side of the swell, our propellers churning and whining until they were back under.

I was long since off the lookout platform, and there wasn't any point to me doing my watch in the sonar room since no U-boat would ever be able to attack in a storm like this. The wolf pack would be running silent and deep, waiting out the storm far below us while we battled the killer waves.

Whatever sea legs guys had grown into over the last couple of weeks were gone now with waves so big. The only good thing was that the ship rode a lot higher in salt water than in freshwater, so when we plunged into the ocean at the bottom of each wave, the bow didn't go as deep as when we went through storms back on Lake Huron, and not quite as much water covered us as we bounced back up.

Chief Kerr called me from the sonar room to the pilot house, where the officers on duty and the navigator ran the ship when weather was too bad for them to be on the bridge, and on the way I realized that once again I was one of the few men on the ship who wasn't doubled over and sick. It was slow going with the howling wind and the waves and the spray. I clipped on a safety line and made my way up to the pilot house with the chief and the executive officer, who didn't look so good, either.

The door slammed so hard behind me that I thought it would take off my leg. I half expected Chief to tell me to take the wheel, but, of course, that wasn't going to happen to a seaman second class with no training—and it didn't. Instead, he wanted me to go back down to the mess and bring back coffee and sandwiches.

I might not have been seasick like most of the rest of the crew, but the idea of eating just then did make my stomach turn. But Chief just yelled the order again and off I went, making my way from the pilot house and down the hatch to the galley, stepping carefully around sailors slumped everywhere—and stepping around where they'd puked, too, which wasn't entirely possible.

In the mess I filled thermoses with black coffee and braced myself as best I could to pull out bread and baloney and anything else I could grab to throw on there, then it was back topside, holding on to the grub with one hand and the rail with the other. Every step seemed to take five minutes as I got thrown side to side, two paces forward, one and a half aft.

I was exhausted by the time I got back to the pilot house but happy I'd finally made it—and been able to do something to help the men who were steering us through this awful storm.

Chief Kerr just cursed and said the coffee had gotten cold. But he ate one whole sandwich in two bites, and then did the same with another one. The executive officer just waved me off. They let me stay in the pilot house, though, and I had a front row seat to the wild climb and fall of the ship up and down those mountainous waves. No turning to run with the wind and the waves as we struggled to keep up with where we at least thought the convoy was. As best I could tell, we were navigating totally with instruments, except when enormous bolts of lightning split the sky in front of us and lit up the way—but only for a second—and then we were plunged back into an even darker night than before until our eyes adjusted.

Chief called me back over to him after another hour. I kind of had an idea about what was coming and I wasn't wrong.

"More coffee, sailor!" he shouted, shoving the thermos into my hands. "And this time get your sorry butt back up here while it's still hot!"

The storm was starting to pass, judging from the size of the waves, which were still high enough to break over the bow, but at least we weren't having to make those steep climbs and gut-punch drops anymore. Just before I climbed back down under the canvas hatch cover to the galley, I saw someone climbing up out of the engine room hatch farther aft on the deck. Lightning crackled overhead, lighting up his face. It was Woody, who I hadn't seen in a couple of days, and not much at all since we'd left New York Harbor a week earlier. That's how it was with the engine room crew—they were like trolls down there in their dark dungeon.

The ship slammed through a wave and water roiled down the length of the ship, knocking Woody off his feet. He wasn't in any danger, but it must have hurt when he landed because he didn't have a life vest on for protection—or to cushion the fall.

"Hey, Woody!" I yelled over the howling wind. I carefully made my way back to check on him, but before I could get there he staggered to his feet and stumbled over to the rail—without a safety line and still without a life vest.

"Stop!" I yelled. "You idiot! It's not safe!"

Woody turned to face me. He must not have known I was there before because his blank face crinkled up into a grin and he lifted his hand to wave, as if we were just on a street somewhere and happened to run into each other, instead of in the middle of a still-raging ocean storm.

I didn't have time to say anything else, because just at that moment, another wave hit the ship and swept Woody over the side!

"Man overboard!" I shouted, as loud as I could. "Man overboard!" And I kept shouting it as I unclipped myself from the safety line, grabbed a life ring, and made my way to the rail. I searched for Woody until I saw him, waving his arms frantically as waves crested over him.

I looked around and saw nobody. I kept yelling for help and started to go find somebody. But I knew if I didn't do something right then and there that Woody wouldn't survive.

I was so scared that I actually wet my pants.

And then, whispering a quick prayer, I jumped over the side of the ship to try to save him.

CHAPTER 15

The shock of landing took my breath away, and I plunged in a lot deeper than I thought I would, so I had to claw my way back up to the surface, still praying the whole time that somebody had heard me shouting. If not, then it didn't matter what happened because Woody and I would both be dead soon in this churning ocean.

More lightning lit up the sky and I saw him between waves, still thrashing wildly, twenty yards away. It was hard to swim with my life vest on and hold on to the ring, but I knew I had to get to Woody fast, as panicked as he was.

Except another wave crashed over us, and then another. I spotted him again, but then he went under all of a sudden. My heart just about stopped until he came back up, trying to

yell but spitting up salt water coughing and gasping. I finally
made it to him and grabbed his arm to hook it over the life
ring, but Woody seemed oblivious to what was happening,
caught up in his panic. He pulled his arm away and flailed
around, nearly hitting me, and then, somehow, he got
behind me and wrapped his arm around my neck, pulling
us both under.

I fought as hard as I could, kicking, twisting, anything to
get away. But Woody was a lot bigger than me, and even
when I was able to pry myself free of his arm, and even with
my life vest on and hanging on to the life ring, the weight of
him on top of me pressed me deeper underwater. I kept
fighting until I managed to wriggle free and kick for the surface, somehow still holding on to the buoy. We probably
hadn't been under for more than half a minute, but I was
desperate for air when I finally came up. I wasn't in the clear
yet, though, because another wave crashed over me as soon
as I got there and I swallowed a lot of water.

Sputtering, I gasped for air and was so scared that I just
wanted to get away from Woody. Before I could get any distance from him, Woody came back up, too—still panicking
and trying to take hold of me again. I was afraid he'd

drown us both this time if he did, especially if he got me around the neck from behind, but I was getting weaker, worn out from being underwater, from the cold, from swallowing so much salt water, and from fighting him off while at the same time trying to hold him up out of the water.

And then out of nowhere, on the other side of a wave, I heard somebody call our names. "Danny! Woody! Where the heck are you guys?"

"Over here!" I yelled. It was Straub. I'd have recognized that big voice anywhere.

The wave crested and suddenly there he was, swimming wildly toward us, splashing so much it was like another wave crashing. Woody was still delirious, though, and grabbed me around the neck yet again, but this time before he could pull me under, Straub was right there with us.

"Oh no you don't!" Straub said, taking hold of Woody's arm. And then, not even hesitating, he punched Woody in the face.

And just like that, the fight went right out of Woody.

I didn't know if the blow knocked him out or if it just stunned him, but he stopped flailing and trying to attack me. He just sort of went limp. Straub and I were able to get him secured to the life ring, and then we both floated on our backs for a minute in the trough of another big wave, buoyed up by our life preservers.

"Didn't think I'd be able to find you guys," Straub said once he caught his breath. "I saw you go over the side and it took me a couple of minutes to find a life preserver."

"Did you see anybody else? Do they know we're out here?" I asked. I started shivering and realized I should have never stopped moving. The water temperature was probably in the fifties, and I was losing body heat fast.

"Pretty sure somebody saw," Straub said, his teeth chattering now, too. "But they have to turn around, and I don't know where these waves have pushed us."

As if on cue, another wave washed over us and we came up sputtering. But it wasn't as big as the one before it, and the next one seemed a little smaller, too.

"We just have to wait," I said. "Thanks for coming. I couldn't have held out much longer. Woody went kind of crazy."

"Poor guy," Straub said. "I guess when you think you're drowning, your brain shuts down on you and you get terrified."

"I guess so," I said, remembering Woody's arm around my neck, and him dragging me underwater and holding me there.

I wasn't through being mad at him, even if he had been out of his mind or whatever.

The good news was the storm kept letting up and the waves kept subsiding to the point where they were no longer crashing over us. The bad news was all the ships were running dark—nobody was even allowed to light a cigarette on deck—so it would be hard to see our patrol craft.

I doubted they would turn on the searchlight because of the wolf pack that was lurking around out there somewhere, maybe waiting for a target.

Ten minutes passed and our teeth were chattering so loud I could hear them. Fifteen minutes passed and Woody slid low into the water, barely holding on to the buoy. It took all my strength to help Straub haul him back up.

Half an hour passed and my heart grew heavy. I couldn't feel my toes and fingers, and I wondered what it would feel like when all three of us slid under, when we didn't have any strength left to hold ourselves up, even with the life vests on. Or would we freeze to death first?

But I couldn't let myself think those thoughts. Straub wasn't going to give up. He was actually humming a song, out of tune. It might have even been "Keep Your Sunny Side Up!" Plus Woody needed me. Mama and Danny needed me.

And then I saw it: a searchlight sweeping over the ocean maybe a quarter mile away. They were still looking for us! I yelled as loud as I could but knew that it was unlikely anybody would hear me over the noise of the engine—if that *was* our ship. The thought occurred to me that it could just as easily be a U-boat, and I stopped yelling. But Straub picked up where I left off with his booming voice.

The ship came closer, and the searchlight swung closer, too, until finally—thank God!—it found us. At that point I didn't care if it was a U-boat or a pirate ship, I was just relieved.

I didn't have to wait long to find out that it was, in fact, our ship. A few minutes later the searchlight was fixed on us, and somebody was throwing a couple more life rings and a line with a harness over the side. Straub and I looped the harness around Woody, who was starting to come out of his stupor, and they hauled him up on board.

Then they threw out the line again, and I fastened the harness on myself the way they'd taught us in boot

He started to say something but got choked up, tears filling his eyes and spilling over down his cheeks.

Straub put his arm around Woody's shoulders. "You don't have to say anything," he said. "Could have happened to any of us. And you'd have been there, jumping in to save us, too."

I nodded. "Yeah. I don't doubt it for a second."

After a minute Woody found his voice. "I know I went kind of crazy out there," he said. "I don't much remember all of it, but I'm ashamed of what I do remember."

Straub waved as if he was swatting the words away like so many flies. "Water under the bridge," he said.

"Or under the patrol craft," I added. "Anyway, one thing I didn't tell you guys was I actually peed on myself when I saw Woody get swept overboard. I figured I had to dive in. Not so much to save Woody as to wash the pee off my pants. That way no one would know."

Straub and Woody broke out laughing. "Well, they're gonna know about it now," Straub said. And that was the end of that.

Except for after my watch, when I climbed down from the observation post like a zombie because I was so tired and

I ran into the chief. He was leaning on the rail looking at the ships strung out in front as far as the eye could see. He motioned me over.

"Yes, Chief?" I said nervously.

He was smoking a pipe. It reminded me of my dad's pipe.

He tamped out the tobacco and ashes and slid the pipe into his pocket. "I don't know what mother back there on land is sitting up nights worrying about her son, but I do know that it's my job to make sure that son—no matter how old he is— makes it home safe from this convoy and this war. Do you understand me?"

I nodded but didn't speak.

"And another thing," he started, then stopped.

"Yes, Chief?" I said again.

He grunted. "That was a heck of a thing you did last night to save your buddy. And a heck of a thing Straub did to save you. I guess if there is a mother back there on land sitting up nights worrying about her son, she'd be an awfully proud one if she knew."

CHAPTER 16

When they let us off the ship for liberty in Key West, Florida, most of the crew headed to the bars, but I went looking for a bank and a post office. Straub and Woody tried to get me to go with them, but I wasn't planning on spending any of my pay. I figured the sooner I cashed my paycheck and mailed off the money to Mama, the less chance there was that I'd change my mind about it. Plus, after two weeks of tight quarters on our little ship, I was ready to just be away from everybody for a few hours, including my pals.

Before I mailed off my pay, I added a letter that was like the other letters. I thought about making up some things that might make Mama happy to read about—like always going to church, singing in the choir, and maybe going to night school after work—but I hated lying to her on top of breaking her heart by leaving the way I did, and her not knowing where I was or anything else about me that was real.

I didn't feel much like that boy who took the dinghy across the sound just a couple of months before and spent the night shivering, curled under the boat. I'd been homesick ever since I left, but I was usually too busy or too tired for it to mess me up. One night up on my bunk I'd started missing Danny so much that I guess I must have made a noise, a big sigh or something, because Straub shot up in his bunk underneath me and asked me what was the matter, were we under attack, did something happen?

"No," I'd whispered, not wanting to wake up anybody else. "I was just missing home is all." Which was true enough.

After I mailed the money home to Mama I wandered around Key West. It wasn't like I had so much as a nickel in my pocket, so there wasn't much of anything I could do. I left the downtown and wandered through a cemetery where all the graves were aboveground, I guess because everything was barely over sea level in Key West. The stones were so white they hurt my eyes. I kept going, down palm-lined streets where people lived in big houses with grand porches and white picket fences. In front of one house, the biggest on Whitehead Street, a couple of cats were out front wrestling with each other. They didn't look too wild, so I bent down to pet them and they let me. One even let me pick him up, and pretty soon he was purring, that cat motor running loud as long as I rubbed his belly. The other cat swam around my legs but didn't want to be picked up—just seemed to want to be close by.

I liked having them with me, and in a few minutes other cats emerged from the shrubs and bushes that surrounded the house and eased their way over to also rub up against my legs. Some let me scratch their heads or behind their ears, or even rub their bellies like the first one. I hadn't ever liked cats that much—the only animal I much cared about back on Ocracoke was my beach pony—but for some reason I liked this a lot.

Then I heard a kid's voice addressing me from the yard. "They've got six toes, you know."

I looked around but couldn't see anybody among the flowering shrubs, banana trees, coconut trees, and palm trees. I knew he was in there somewhere, though.

"Count them if you don't believe me," the kid added.

I counted the cat's toes and sure enough there were six on each foot.

"Pretty strange, huh?" said the kid, standing up and wading through the bushes and the flowers. He was about my age—my real age, not the age I was pretending to be.

"Yeah," I said. "I've never seen anything like it. Are they all that way?"

The kid sat down beside me in the grass.

"Most of them. A ship captain gave that one to Papa. Her name is Snow White. I guess they're all freaks. But they'll still let you pet them."

The kid said his name was Patrick and he asked how old I was, and for some reason I gave him my real age.

"That's how old I am, too," he said. "But you're in the navy. How did you join? Papa told me you have to be seventeen to sign up."

"I might have fibbed some about my age," I said. "You can't tell anybody."

Patrick waved away the suggestion. "Ah, who would I tell? Anyway, Papa's coming to get me pretty soon on his boat and he's taking me back to Cuba where he lives, and him and me are going to go hunting U-boats. You know about U-boats? That's the German submarines."

I had to laugh. Did I know about U-boats? They were all I'd been thinking about for the past three months!

"So you and your dad are going to go after the U-boats in, what, a fishing boat or something?"

"Deep-sea fishing boat," Patrick said. "Papa says we'll radio the navy when we spot one, and they'll come over from the base they have in Cuba and blow it up. Plus Papa has rifles."

"A rifle isn't going to do you any good against a submarine," I said.

"Do you know who my papa is?" Patrick said, as if that was any kind of answer.

I shook my head. "How would I?"

"He's Ernest Hemingway," Patrick said. "You know who that is, don't you?"

"Sure," I said, surprised but trying not to sound like it. "Ernest Hemingway the author. Everybody's heard of him." I didn't mention that I'd never read any of Ernest Hemingway's books.

"He used to live here in Key West with us, but he doesn't anymore," Patrick said, looking kind of sad. "He married somebody else."

I didn't know what to say about that, so I just kept petting Snow White.

"Hey, you want to go swimming in our pool?" Patrick asked.

I'd never met anybody with their own swimming pool before. The only pools I'd ever seen, in fact, were the giant ones at Great Lakes and in Miami at the training centers. There sure weren't any on Ocracoke Island.

I followed Patrick through the jungle of a yard, the cats still swarming around us the whole time, to the back of the big house, where there was a huge rectangular pool filled with blue water. "There's some extra trunks in the house," Patrick said. "I'll get you some. Come on."

A few minutes later I was out of my navy whites and into a pair of swimming trunks that I had to cinch around my waist with a piece of string to keep them from falling down. And then off we went back to the pool, which turned out to be salt water, because there was no freshwater on Key West except for rainwater they caught in cisterns, as Patrick helpfully explained.

"Let's do depth charges," he ordered.

"Depth charges?" I repeated.

"Yeah, you know, what they shoot off ships to blow up U-boats."

I told him I knew what depth charges were, and that we had them on our patrol craft and fired them off with something called a K-gun. I was just wondering what he meant when he asked me if I wanted *do* depth charges.

"Like cannonballs," Patrick said, and he ran toward the pool and jumped as high as he could go and grabbed his knees, curling his head and shoulders forward just before he landed and made a giant splash.

"Right," I said, and I did it, too.

As soon as I came up, somebody else cannonballed into the Hemingways' pool, too, yelling "Geronimo!" on the way down.

It was a boy wearing what looked like a girl's swimming suit.

Patrick rolled his eyes. "That's my little brother. We call him Gigi. He likes to wear stuff like that. Don't ask me why."

Gigi just grinned. I shrugged and we all climbed out and did it again, this time yelling "Bombs away!" every time we did a cannonball. After about half an hour, a woman who I guess was their servant or their maid came out with a tray with three big glasses of lemonade and a plate of cookies. I didn't even wait to be invited. I drank one of the lemonades in one giant gulp and would have eaten every single cookie if Patrick and Gigi hadn't jumped out of the pool and joined me and stuffed some in their mouths, too.

It was the funnest time I'd had since Danny got hurt, and even though our bellies were totally full from the lemonade and cookies, we didn't wait an hour before we went back in the water like you were supposed to. There were U-boats down in the bottom of that pool and we were the depth charges that were going to sink them for good, so no time to waste!

A lady looked out at us a couple of times from an upstairs window in their house. Patrick said it was their mom and she didn't come outside very much. She waved to us and I waved back and then she disappeared. I thought of my mom, and how sad she was for a long time after we lost my dad, and wondered how much it was like that for Mrs. Hemingway, even though her husband hadn't passed away. He was still gone, though, married to a different lady, so maybe it was the same.

Patrick and Gigi and I played in their swimming pool pretty much the whole rest of the afternoon, interrupted every now and then by their servant coming out with more lemonade, and sometimes we climbed out to chase six-toed cats around their yard. It sure was nice getting to be a kid again.

Finally, though, it was time for me to change back into my uniform and go back on board my ship.

Little Gigi, still wearing his girl's swimsuit, gave me a book just before I left—one their father had written recently called *For Whom the Bell Tolls.* Then he ran off. Patrick walked with me halfway down the street toward the docks.

"That book, it's about an American guy in Spain who is fighting the fascists," he said. "They're like the Spanish Nazis. Mama won't let us read it, but I bet you'll like it. Papa's the best writer there is."

"Thanks," I said. "Good luck hunting U-boats with your dad down in Cuba."

I thought about them in just a fishing boat, with a radio and a rifle, and I added, "Be safe."

"You too," Patrick said.

We shook hands like grown-ups.

CHAPTER 17

We didn't run into any trouble crossing the Straits of Florida, the sort of dividing line between the Gulf of Mexico and the Atlantic Ocean, which took us back to the shipping lanes for the return trip up the East Coast. Lieutenant Talley must have gotten some kind of warning in Key West, because he seemed worried and walked the deck constantly, confirming everybody's positions, double-checking weapons and ammo, haunting the sonar room. I half expected him to climb up to the lookout platform where I spent most of my watches. He stood on the bridge and stared at me a lot, though, as if just waiting for me to sight something and initiate the call to general quarters.

The merchant ships were loaded with tons of sugar and bananas and coffee and frozen meats from all around the Caribbean and South America, bound for New York and then probably with another convoy over to England. There were also dozens of civilians whose passenger ship had been sunk by U-boats out in the Caribbean the week before. Only half of those on board had survived. My heart sank watching them board the ship for the voyage back north. All they had was the clothes they were wearing and blankets. Everything else they owned must have been lost when their ship went down—along with their friends and their families. Their faces looked drained of color. Nobody smiled. Hardly any of them spoke. They trudged up the gangway as if they were going away to prison.

We were halfway up the Florida coast when word came from the sonar room that there were U-boats stalking the convoy. Our patrol craft was the usual blur of activity as everybody raced to battle stations. I was in the crow's nest and warned the other ships about the danger with the signal flags because we'd been maintaining radio silence since leaving port.

A minute later our PC surged ahead, peeling off from the convoy to where the sonar guys had spotted a U-boat lying in wait. So far I hadn't seen a thing, but I trained my binoculars ahead, hoping to see something that might help.

One of the other PCs on our side of the convoy took off as well in pursuit of a second U-boat, while the third escort stayed on course. All the ships increased their speed, but that still wasn't very fast with all the cargo they carried. They also began the zigzag pattern to make it at least a little harder for the U-boats to aim their torpedoes, though as slow as they traveled it was hard to believe it would help very much.

After five minutes giving chase, Lieutenant Talley issued another order and the battery crew launched a couple of depth charges. I held on to the rail, bracing myself for the blast, and once again it felt as if the ship was lifted high out of the water, landing with such force that it was a wonder we didn't break apart right then and there. No sooner did we settle than the second depth charge went off. I was grinding my teeth so hard that my jaw ached.

Oil and debris came to the surface, and guys all over the PC started shouting that we'd made a direct hit. They were practically dancing all over the deck until Chief Kerr jumped off the bridge and stormed up and down yelling at them all to knock it off. "Back to your stations!" he bellowed. "We didn't hit nothing! It's an old sub trick!"

I remembered the training back in Miami and he was right. U-boats had been known to intentionally release oil, mattresses, and clothes through their torpedo chutes—anything that might convince us that they'd been hit. But what they were really doing was either getting away, or hiding on the bottom, or lining up for another torpedo shot—maybe even at the ship that was in pursuit.

Maybe even at us.

Lieutenant Talley ordered another depth charge launched, and we went through the whole thing again, only no more oil and no more debris came up this time, so it probably *had* been a case of the U-boat pulling a trick and getting away, like Chief said. And it had worked. It was the third time we'd chased a U-boat, and we still didn't have anything to show for it.

As we pulled back toward the convoy I could see the other PC far forward of our position still in pursuit of the second U-boat. They must have spotted something because they seemed to be giving chase. I wondered where the others in the wolf pack might be, and suddenly I had my terrible answer as an explosion erupted at the fantail of one of the merchant ships, an arc of fire shooting up like a rocket. Seconds later there was another explosion farther forward on the ship, and more flames and smoke billowed up into the clear afternoon sky.

It was the same ship all the civilians were on! I couldn't believe it was happening to them again. The escort PC that had stayed back with the convoy fired its cannon at the spot where the torpedoes had first been spotted as we raced back to join them in defending the cargo ships. The one that had been hit listed hard to starboard, and I could see the lifeboats being lowered and people climbing in. The air smelled like diesel fuel and burning oil. Small bits of metal debris rained down on us, and I had to climb from the crow's nest to safety.

We all wanted to go help the survivors—it was a rescue operation now—but we still had to be wary of the rest of the wolf pack, and soon we were off again in pursuit of yet another U-boat. I joined one of the battery crews this time, loading shells into the forward cannon, and we flew over the water at full throttle, hammering the tops of the waves but not slowing down. Behind us, the other cargo ships were taking on the survivors, and the second PC was returning from what must have been a failed U-boat pursuit.

This time we weren't going to miss our target. Lieutenant Talley gave the order to reverse engines to slow us down once we got to a certain point, near enough to the U-boat we were chasing, according to our sonar, and then we unleashed everything—depth charges from the K- and Y-guns, rocket bombs from Hedgehogs. Explosions blew geysers a hundred feet in the air all around us, and our PC rocked wildly. Guys were flung around worse than in the storm a week earlier. Damage control crews raced belowdecks again. And gunnery crews kept at the ready in case a U-boat surfaced and we could use the deck guns on it.

Behind us, the wounded cargo ship rolled farther onto its side, and then, with a loud groan and the grinding sound of twisting metal, broke in half. Both halves went down within minutes, and I prayed that everyone had gotten off safely—especially the survivors from before.

We repaired damaged bulkheads and reloaded the depth charges and rocket bombs. We stared at the ocean, the water calmer now that the explosions were over. We studied the sonar, pinging off what had to be a sub, now motionless below us. And we waited to see what would come up from the bottom.

"What do you think?" Straub asked me, as the waiting stretched on for what felt like an hour.

We were back at the forward gun, the 3"/50-caliber, ready with more shells.

I'd just come up from the sonar room. "It's not moving, and it's definitely a sub," I said. "Just can't tell from the sonar if we hit it."

"Concussion from the depth charges and those rockets could have blown bolts out, could have caused leaks all over that U-boat," the gunnery chief said. "They could be drowned inside of there."

I shuddered at the thought of that. Then I shuddered at the thought of any of the submarine crew dying in any way under the ocean.

"I hope they *are* all dead," I muttered, though I knew in my heart I didn't mean it. I didn't know why, either. For months all I had wanted was revenge for what they'd done to Danny. But now that there was a pretty good chance we'd sunk a sub, I hated the thought of a whole crew of men who were alive just half an hour ago now being, well, not alive. What if it had been our ship that had been hit by a torpedo instead—and what if we were all trapped on board as we sank?

"I don't know," Straub said. "I kind of hope they surface and just surrender and we take them prisoner. That way they're out of the war for good, but, you know, we didn't kill them or anything."

"Only good Kraut is a dead Kraut," said another guy on our crew. I knew *Kraut* was something they called German people, but Mama wouldn't ever let Danny and me use a word like that.

I said maybe Straub was right, but even as I said it, I wasn't so sure I believed that, either. I wanted to bury all the Germans and their U-boats. But at the same time I didn't want them to die. It was so complicated.

Maybe what I wanted was for everything to just be back the way it was with Mama and Dad and Danny and me, and nobody trying to blow anybody up in the ocean anymore, and no crazy, stupid war.

CHAPTER 18

Suddenly, bubbles started rising to the surface, a lot of bubbles, and the water began moving, churning, frothing.

"It's coming up!" Straub shouted. "Look there!"

And sure enough, a dark shape emerged from the depths, rising little by little into the space where the sunlight penetrated down into the water. The higher the shape rose, the more distinct it became, with a clearer outline and color. The bow. The forward deck gun. The tower. Finally, the deck— though not high enough to clear the waves.

It must have been damaged, because that was as far as the U-boat could surface. The hatch opened on the tower, and we saw hands first—raised hands as a German sailor climbed out and onto the deck, where he had to stand in a good foot of water. The waves continued to roll over the deck and around his legs, and the legs of the sailor who followed him, and the one after that and the one after that. Soon, the whole crew was standing, lined up with their hands in the air, and then the officers emerged.

They were directly port side of our ship. Half of our crew was perched along the rail, rifles and machine guns aimed and ready. Straub and I stayed with the big deck cannon, though we were too close to the sub to fire at it if anything happened.

Lieutenant Talley shouted something from the bridge—in German, which surprised me. I didn't think any of us knew he spoke the language.

"Probably learned it in college," Straub said.

Somebody told him to shut up so we could hear.

The captain kept speaking in German, and an officer, who I guess was the U-boat captain, answered him. I whispered to Straub, asking if he knew what they were saying, but he shook his head and whispered back that his parents didn't want him to learn it. "Probably so they could talk about me when I was in the same room, but I wouldn't know what they were saying," he joked.

Somebody shushed him again.

Lieutenant Talley and the German officer talked for a while longer, and then a couple of the U-boat crew members broke ranks and climbed down the hatch back into the sub. They returned a few minutes later with one of their crew, clearly injured, strapped to a stretcher, and they handed him off to others on the deck. The sailors on deck couldn't put the stretcher anywhere because of the waves, so they just held him there, swaying as the sub rocked, a couple of times scrambling to keep their balance. The injured submariner's face was filthy with smoke or grease, and I wondered if he'd been in their engine room. It made me think of Woody.

The Germans brought up three more stretchers one by one, with more injured crew members. One was covered in blood, but at least he was still alive. There was a sheet pulled over the face of the last man they brought out. All the German sailors pulled off their caps and bowed their heads.

Half an hour later, the U-boat crew—all living except the one—were on board our ship, sitting in a tight circle near the stern, with several of our crew, me included, standing watch over them with our weapons. I felt important, but at the same time I also felt like I didn't belong there, that I would never be able to shoot my rifle at anybody—and definitely not at any of the German U-boat crew, even knowing that they might have been the ones who sank one of our ships. They just looked young and scared.

The captain ordered water for them and we brought them water. He ordered food for them and we brought them the lousiest food we could find—stale bread, meat that was going bad, some black bananas. I didn't feel sorry enough for them that I was going to give away anything very edible, especially since we had even more survivors on our side now we had to take care of.

The engineers got to work hooking cables from our stern to the bow of the sub so we could tow it back to Key West. But then we got a message to sink it instead. The navy didn't want us to waste any more time on this voyage than we had to and risk being unnecessary targets for the remaining U-boats. We would take the prisoners with us.

A boarding party went over from our PC and stripped all the communications equipment along with any and every-thing else that might be useful. They might have also rifled through the German submariners' personal effects, because later one guy showed me a wallet filled with German money, not that it was probably going to do him any good. Unless he thought Germany was going to win the war.

Once they finished and came back, the engineers cut the cables. Our PC backed off several hundred yards. Then the gunnery chief aimed the big gun and we fired—and missed.

Too high.

So we loaded another shell and fired again and missed again.

This time too low.

The third time we scored a direct hit and an enormous explosion split the U-boat in half. A couple of the German sailors gasped. Some shook their heads in what looked like despair. One even started silently weeping.

The U-boat sank faster than our cargo ship had a few hours earlier, but it was a lot smaller. In fact I was surprised at how small it was. In my mind, the one that attacked me and Danny had been gigantic, the size of a whale, like Moby Dick.

Just before we rejoined the convoy we got the good news: Everyone on the merchant ship had gotten off safely before it sank, though several were injured and needed medical treatment. The other cargo ships were now crowded, with the survivors mostly huddled on deck—the same as us with all our prisoners—but we cheered anyway. All the explosions, all the depth charges and the rockets and the shells and the torpedoes, and only one person, that German sailor with the sheet drawn over his face, had died.

"I think it's a miracle," Straub said.

Somebody else, one of the older guys on the crew, just laughed. "Wasn't nothing but pure dumb luck," he said. "Just pure dumb luck. Another time, another torpedo, another depth charge, another ten feet this way or that, and either we could have all been dead or they could have all been dead. You go along thinking your life is something so special—until you learn the hard truth that in war it just ain't."

The U-boats weren't finished with us yet. The rest of the wolf pack kept following us up the Florida coast. We'd see traces of them—a glimpse of a periscope, the wake of one that just dove under, some faint pings on the sonar. They bided their time when we pulled into Jacksonville to drop off our prisoners and the cargo ship survivors. They were still out there when we left Jacksonville to continue on up the coast back to New York.

Another storm kept them away for a couple of days, but then it got calm again, and clear, with a full moon at night and no clouds, which meant we had to be more vigilant than ever as the convoy crawled slowly north.

We spotted one, gave chase, and lost it. One of the other PCs guarding the other side of the convoy chased U-boats twice, though they didn't get close enough to fire cannon or launch rocket bombs or depth charges.

"How can they stay out so long?" I asked Chief Kerr. "I mean, don't they have to refuel some time?"

It was a night watch and we were leaning on the rail below the bridge, feeling, more than seeing, the ocean splitting in two as the bow sliced through the water and waves rushed under and around us. There was a soft rolling motion that if I was in my bunk just then would have put me right to sleep, no matter how bad it smelled down there.

"I guess they didn't teach you about the milch cows," he said.

"What's that?" I asked.

"Special subs the Germans designed that they send out to rendezvous points around the Atlantic. They meet up with the wolf packs to refuel and rearm them with more torpedoes so they don't have to go all the way back to their bases in Europe, which can take weeks. So, milch cows."

Then he added, as if he didn't think I could figure it out on my own, "*Milch* means 'milk' in German."

We were running dark the way we always did at night, relying on visual contact to keep the ships from coming too close to one another—and hoping we were hidden well enough that the wolf pack wouldn't be able to see us to aim and fire their torpedoes. But there was nothing we could do about the full moon, except keep to a zigzag course with the entire convoy. The problem with that was it slowed us down even more and might have even made us easier targets. But it was the ranking officer on one of the other PCs who got to make the decision and we followed it, though Chief Kerr kept spitting and cursing, not pleased with what we were doing.

"Full speed ahead is what I say," he fumed. "Those cargo ships might not go fast, but they can sure go fast*er*."

Other than saying those things to me, though, I was pretty sure the chief kept his opinions to himself.

CHAPTER 19

On the second dogwatch, I met up with Woody for dinner, which was canned meat and gravy over boiled potatoes, and something green next to it that might or might not have been a vegetable. We just called it evening slime.

Woody smelled pretty rank as usual, and his clothes—and face and hands—were grease-stained. He didn't bother washing up but just dove right into the food, which he obviously enjoyed a lot more than the rest of us. I picked at mine and mostly ate crackers and drank coffee, even though Mama wouldn't ever let me have it back home because she said it would stunt my growth. Nobody said that here, and I figured if there was one thing I did that she wouldn't approve of, better drinking coffee than a lot of other stuff.

"Nice to get out of that engine room once in a while," Woody said between bites. "You know how tight it is back there? And I'm not just talking about the engine room, either. I'm talking about where we all bunk. It's a good thing everybody gets along."

"You sound like you actually like it," I said.

Woody nodded. "You know, I kind of do. I've even been thinking that after the war—you know, after we kick Germany's butt and everything—I might even stay in the navy." He held up a forkful of evening slime. "They feed you, give you a place to sleep, teach you a job, and you get a paycheck once a month that you can spend however you want. Can't see what's not to like about it."

Another guy sitting with us in the mess scoffed. His name was Fulton. "What about getting yourself killed by a torpedo? I can see a lot that's not to like about that."

"Hasn't happened so far," Woody said, reaching over to scrape my uneaten canned meat and slime onto his plate. "Plus where I'm from, you could get run over by a tractor, stomped on by a horse, all kinds of things. You could spend your whole life cropping tobacco on somebody else's tobacco farm and not have anything to show for it. I don't mind taking my chances on a little ship like this, running up and down the East Coast, getting to go to those bars down in Key West. And I bet they got some good ones in New York City, too. I hope we get liberty up there once we deliver this convoy back safe and sound."

"Here's hoping that happens," I said. "We already lost one ship."

"Yeah, but we got one of theirs back," Woody said. "Bet that's why they're staying away."

Fulton scoffed again. "They ain't staying away, farm boy. They're just waiting for us to let our guard down."

Woody shrugged and swallowed his last bite of my dinner. "I still like it here," he said.

Later that same night I was back on the lookout platform. It was midwatch, two in the morning, that full moon high above us casting short shadows off the ships. The white foam behind the fantail was practically shining. The PC was quiet, but I knew the whole crew was being vigilant since we were so exposed. It might as well have been daytime, except that then I'd at least have had a chance of seeing a glint of sunlight off a periscope lens letting me know that we had U-boat company. I knew they were out there, just like Fulton said down in the mess earlier, waiting for us to make a mistake.

Well, if anybody did make one, it wasn't going to be me.

I doubled my efforts, scanning the horizon with the binoculars and without, straining to pick up any sign of U-boat activity. They often surfaced at night and rode high in the water like any other ship. I doubted they would do that on a night like this when visibility was so strong, though.

The minutes ticked by slower than I could ever remember, and I kept getting more and more anxious, practically giving myself whiplash turning my head and trying to see everywhere all at once, not wanting to miss anything.

And then I saw it—a torpedo maybe a quarter mile away coming right at us, lit up by phosphorus in the water so it gleamed silver. I sounded the alarm and yelled down to the bridge to take evasive action NOW! The squawk box barked out the order and the engines roared. We shot ahead and then hard to starboard, nearly spinning in a circle, like a matador fighting a bull. The torpedo kept racing right at us and I couldn't see how it would miss—until it did! We had pulled just enough ahead, and swung around just enough, that it shot right past us and continued harmlessly out into the ocean—thankfully not hitting any of the other ships.

The call went out to general quarters and as guys ran to their posts our PC swung all the way around and now raced in the direction the torpedo had come from. I was still in the crow's nest and the first to see a second torpedo also coming straight at us. I yelled down to the bridge again and this time it was easier to dodge.

We continued on to where the U-boat must've been, not waiting to get there before the order came to fire the cannon, even though we couldn't see the target. But it had to be ahead of us somewhere, and fairly close by. The shells exploded, sending those giant plumes of water up into the night sky like silver fountains in the moonlight.

"Prepare depth charges!" the captain barked over the squawk box as we pressed on, our PC going so fast we seemed to be skimming the tops of the waves again.

There was no time to climb down from the lookout platform, so I held on as tight as I could and might have been the only one to see the third torpedo, just before it hit.

The explosion was on our starboard side, and it threw me so hard against the rail that I would have gone over and fallen to the bridge if my safety line hadn't been attached. I must have hit my head because I blacked out for a minute— it had to have only been a minute, because when I regained consciousness the ship was still rocking wildly from the explosion.

I dragged myself up and looked down at the ship, where guys were also picking themselves up and going back to their stations. I expected to see torn metal, fires, all kinds of destruction, but the damage must have been under the ship somewhere. And since we weren't listing to the side I hoped it wasn't too bad, maybe not a direct hit.

Next thing I knew we were firing back at the U-boat with everything we had. Maybe someone had gotten a sonar ping or visual sighting. My vision had been okay at first, but now I was having a hard time seeing. Something was covering my face, and when I wiped it away, I realized it was my own blood pouring from a gash on my forehead.

More explosions threw me down again—from the depth charges and the rockets—and this time I stayed down, both hands pressed against the wound to stop the bleeding. Something happened, maybe we scored a hit, because there was more firing—machine guns on the aft deck—which meant we had been in a firefight with the U-boat. Which meant the U-boat had surfaced and was fighting rather than surrendering the way the other one had done.

I tried to get up but must have lost too much blood because I felt faint and sagged back down onto the lookout platform, my legs too weak for me to stand. But I wanted to be down there. I wanted to be helping. I wanted to be shooting guns at those Germans and protecting my friends and my ship.

Engines revved and the PC jerked into motion—away from the battle. I heard another engine and that must have been the U-boat doing the same thing. Both ships were damaged, including, I found out later, our big gun, which was why we couldn't use it in the face-off, and both ships were retreating. I kept hoping I would see the U-boat sink, but it just kept pulling away from us until it was out of sight and out of range.

I managed to drag myself down from the lookout platform, though my hands kept slipping because of all the blood. I still don't know how I managed it. When I got to the bridge, I collapsed again, but everything was so chaotic on the ship that nobody noticed at first. Others had been wounded, and the officers and crew were scrambling to help them, and to shore up leaks in the bulkhead, and to make repairs down in the engine room. Oily smoke billowed up from somewhere below.

And then I blacked out again.

I must have been out for quite a while, because when I woke up I was belowdecks in my bunk. It took me a few minutes to figure that out. My head was heavy with bandages wrapped around me like a turban. There was still blood all over the front of my uniform, but it was dried.

Two sailors were talking in low voices nearby, but I only heard part of what they were saying.

"Some guy in the engine room . . . Pipe burst . . . Killed instantly."

Right away I thought about Woody and tried to sit up—to go find him, to make sure he was okay and it wasn't him they were talking about—but I was too weak. I collapsed back onto my bunk. My heart raced, and there was a pounding in my head that felt as if it was going to split my skull in two.

"Hey now," one of the sailors said. "Easy there, buddy. Just lie back down there. You got hurt pretty bad. You can't be getting up."

"Was it Woody?" I whispered. My mouth was so dry, my throat parched, that I could barely speak.

One of the guys gave me some water. Then I asked again about Woody, my heart sinking at the thought of him gone.

But it wasn't him. Woody, they said, had been a hero. One man had died in the engine room when the torpedo partially blew in the side of the ship, but Woody had saved two others.

"He pulled them out to safety," one of the guys said. "Burned his hands going back for the second one, too."

I couldn't believe it. The guy who didn't know his right from his left, who had the words tattooed on his arms so he could remember, who conked himself out walking into a pipe in the engine room his first day on the ship, who got so hysterical that he nearly drowned me, and Straub had to knock him out when we went overboard—that same guy had known exactly what to do in the emergency. Not only dragging those two men to safety, burning his hands in the process, but, as I later found out, also going back a third time to put out the engine room fire and staying to help shore up leaks from the blast.

"That farm boy," one of the sailors said, shaking his head. "You never know who's going to come through in a situation like that. Some'll just freeze on you. But some, like him, well, it's good to have him on our side, I can tell you that."

I must have slept after that, or just drifted back into unconsciousness. When I came to again, head still pounding but not quite as bad, Woody and Straub were there.

"About time you opened your eyes," Straub said. "We were just about to give up on you. Figured we might have to do one of those burials at sea."

"Nah," Woody said, waving his bandaged hands. "We're just glad you're okay. They think you might have a concussion. Nice cut on your head you got there, too. Lots of blood."

"Yeah," said Straub. "Better take it easy. But they said you could be up and about in a couple of days. Nothing that won't heal right up."

"I heard somebody in the engine room got, uh . . ." I couldn't finish.

Woody nodded solemnly. "It was Big Carrot. The chief motor machinist's mate. He was standing right next to where the torpedo hit and caught the full force of it."

Woody shook his head, as if he couldn't quite get his mind all the way around what had just happened. He didn't seem upset—I guessed that would come later. He just seemed bewildered. Confused. Lost.

"They got a couple more of our guys, too," Straub said. "That guy Fulton you were just having dinner with. He caught some metal in his side and bled out. But I'm pretty sure we got a lot more of theirs than they got of ours."

I started crying then. I couldn't help it. The tears came on their own and I couldn't stop them, no matter how hard I tried. I turned my face away from Woody and Straub, toward the hull, and wished I was back home on Ocracoke Island, back in my own house, in my own bed, with my own family. Woody and Straub patted me on the shoulder and left me alone to cry myself back to sleep.

CHAPTER 20

By the time we pulled into New York Harbor I was back at my duty station on regular watch, but there were no more encounters with the wolf pack—no sightings, no nothing. Our PC was able to limp along, keeping pace with the lumbering ships in the convoy, but because of the damage to the hull we weren't in any shape to chase U-boats. But we could at least pretend, so that was what we did.

There was no way to transport the three men who'd been killed—Big Carrot, Fulton, and a seaman named Cissel—so Lieutenant Talley ordered them buried at sea. I was still too weak from my head wound so I didn't have to assist, but I watched as other guys placed the bodies in long canvas sacks with weights at their feet and tied tight at the top. They were laid on planks, and the planks carried to the side of the ship. Lieutenant Talley said a prayer for each man, and then a couple of sailors who volunteered—Straub was one of them—tipped the planks up so that the bodies slid off and into the ocean and disappeared.

It was a scene that stayed with me for days, for the whole rest of the trip—those canvas bags in the shape of the dead men's bodies. The way they went into the water feetfirst, as if they were standing at attention, which I guessed they would be once the weights carried them down to the bottom. It was hard to feel anything except sad. Woody seemed to be the same as me whenever I saw him, which wasn't often since they were down two men in the engine room and everybody had to work extra watches. We would sit quietly together in the mess, drinking coffee and eating stuff from cans, if either of us had an appetite. It was strange to see him like that. It was strange for both of us to feel like we were suddenly a lot older than we'd been just the week before.

And a whole lot older than we'd been just three months earlier, riding that bus to Illinois for basic training.

Neither one of us had much stomach for going into the city for shore leave, either, even though Straub tried his best to cheer us up and get us to go with him. "We can catch a baseball game!" he said. "Eat hot dogs! All kinds of stuff! It's New York City!"

Finally, we gave in and went with him, and surprised ourselves by having a good time at the Polo Grounds. I'd never been to a real professional baseball game before. Afterward, I couldn't even remember who was playing—besides the Giants, of course. I was a Washington Senators fan since they were the closest team to Ocracoke, but it was just from reading about them in the newspaper, which always came out a week after the games. There was something kind of nice about being in that big crowd of people yelling and clapping and whistling, and cursing when something bad happened, and drinking and eating, and not caring about a thing in the world except a ball game.

I saw Woody smiling at one point, probably for the first time in a week, and laughing at something Straub said. I got so tired after the seventh-inning stretch that the guys told me I fell asleep in my seat and missed the rest of the game, but I didn't really care. It turned out to be the best hour of sleep I'd had in weeks.

For the rest of the summer that was our life: escorting convoys up and down the East Coast, sometimes back to Key

West but usually farther, to New Orleans or even Texas. The New Orleans and Texas runs were all about protecting oil tankers from U-boats in the Gulf of Mexico and made us especially nervous, because if one of them got hit by a torpedo, there was an enormous explosion, the whole ship erupting into a giant fireball, even the ocean around the ship on fire. There usually weren't any survivors. And the ones that did survive didn't survive for long. They'd be choking on oil when we fished them out of the ocean, coughing up black gunk, not able to speak, and after a while—a short while—not able to breathe.

We lost three tankers over the next three months, but it seemed like every trip, every convoy, we encountered fewer and fewer U-boats. Never as many as we did on that first convoy. We didn't sink any more, but we chased plenty of them off. Chief said it looked like they were staying farther away, only venturing in close enough to fire their torpedoes at night, and usually when there was some moonlight. So that wasn't too often. By late September, we had two successive runs without seeing a single U-boat.

"Hardly seems like they need us anymore," Straub said as we neared New York Harbor at the end of that second run.

"I guess better safe than sorry," I said. "Sure does seem like maybe we did it, though—chased them off from the East Coast."

"Gotta give some credit to the spotter planes," Straub said, which was true.

"And the blackout," I added, which was also true. All up and down the coast, from small towns to the biggest cities, people were putting out lights or covering up windows at night, like we'd done on Ocracoke, so the U-boats couldn't see cargo ships' silhouettes against the shoreline, and so no more easy targets.

"You think they'll pull us off this duty and put us to use somewhere else?" Straub asked. There were a couple of other guys in the mess with us, but they just shrugged. We'd been working nonstop for months, with only a few days of liberty after that one long weekend in New York when we went to the baseball game while the ship was repaired. Everybody was dog-tired.

"I heard they're moving closer to sending off that invasion force, and they're going to need ships to transport our troops over to, well, wherever we end up attacking," I said. "France, I guess. Or Belgium. Or Italy."

The army, navy, and marines were fighting the Japanese all over the Pacific, but other than continuing to supply the Soviets and the British with food and weapons, we still hadn't sent troops to Europe to fight the Nazis and the Axis powers. Everybody kept saying it was about to happen, but nobody seemed to know exactly when or where.

"I don't know," Straub said. "They'll need transport ships for the invasion. And they'll have battleships and destroyers and aircraft carriers. What would they need a bunch of little bathtubs like ours for?"

One of the guys sitting there with us started quacking. The other guy joined him.

I had to laugh. "Yeah, Donald Duck Navy. That's still us."

I wasn't ready to give up on the idea that we might have a role to play in the invasion force, though. "They're going to need us PCs," I said. "Maybe for reconnaissance. Or maybe as command ships. Definitely to rescue survivors when any of those troop transports get torpedoed."

"You're dreaming, Danny," one of the quacking guys said. "Once we're done running off the U-boats, they'll probably mothball our entire little fleet of PCs and send us all to typing school."

Chief walked into the mess just then and must have heard our conversation because he weighed in on it right away.

"They've gone north," he said.

"Who has, Chief?" Straub asked.

"The U-boats," Chief said. "Or haven't you noticed they're not around anymore?"

"Well, sure we have," Straub said. "So what now?"

"So we go north, too," Chief said. "Orders just came in. Wolf packs are all over the north passage now that they're not down here anymore. The last convoy across reported eighty U-boat attacks. Lost a dozen ships. So they need us up there. We'll be escorting convoys over to England. Maybe to the USSR. Out of Newfoundland."

We just looked at him for a minute. I guess none of us were too good with geography.

"It's in Canada," Chief said, shaking his head. "You boys will get to see Iceland. And Greenland. We'll pass them on the way over. Assuming we make it that far. Won't have air support for most of the passage."

"I've never been out of America before," one of the quacking guys said. "Wonder what it'll be like."

Chief snorted. "Just like here, only different. But don't worry. You'll be too busy fighting those bad ocean storms they got up there to notice, not to mention all those wolf packs. And did I mention how cold it's gonna get? Ice and snow like you wouldn't believe."

He chuckled. "Other than that, though, a picnic."

Two weeks later, everything that Chief had told us was going to happen, happened. We pulled out of Newfoundland as one of a dozen escort ships—six PCs, a couple of destroyers, and four British corvette warships, which were like their version of our patrol crafts. Our job was to protect a hundred ships riding low across the North Atlantic with everything you could think of for the war effort in England—meat, cereals, lubricating oils, machinery, wood, paper, chemicals, iron ore, minerals, cement, guns, tanks, even planes.

Lieutenant Talley addressed us from the bridge as the massive convoy steamed out of port. "You men have heard the rumors and they're all true. The German U-boats have left the shipping lanes along the East Coast, and you were an important part of chasing them away. But now they're swarming all over the North Atlantic route we'll be taking, and it's our job to see to it that they don't sink a single one of the ships in this convoy. England's ability to continue holding out against the Nazis until we can get our American troops over there to bail them out is riding on this mission. From what I understand, that is still some months away. So it's up to us. It's up to *you*. To make sure what's on these cargo ships makes it across safely to the people who desperately need it to survive."

He paused and I was struck by how much older Lieutenant Talley seemed, just like the rest of us, compared to the first time I saw him on our voyage out on Lake Huron for the shakedown cruise. Nobody would joke about him being a college boy now. In just these past several months, he'd turned into as hard an officer as any of them.

"The way I see it," he continued, "and the way you should see it, is that not only are we responsible for getting these supplies over to England to save the people there, we're also responsible for getting these supplies over to England to help save the world from the Nazis."

CHAPTER 21

We were the caboose—the last ship in the convoy, charged with protecting against any U-boat attacks from the rear. It was an impossible job, with so many ships, and so much ocean, and so few of us PCs and corvettes and even with the two destroyers, especially as we hit a storm almost as soon as we left port that spread the convoy out over miles and reduced visibility to just about zero.

For two days we sailed into a gale force wind so strong that our PC literally made no headway at all. Radio contact was limited, but from what we could tell, the cargo ships were able to move forward, though slowly, along with the destroyers. The PCs and corvettes, light as we were, would have to play catch-up once the wind died down.

Except when the wind died, we were hit with an early snow of all things, temperatures dropping so low that ice formed everywhere on the ship. Somebody said the deck was slick enough that you could ice-skate on it, though with the still-rough ocean bouncing us around you'd ice-skate right off the side and turn into a human ice cube as soon as you hit the water.

About the only members of the crew allowed topside were the officers on the bridge and the navigators. It was just too dangerous for the rest of us, and we had to figure it was too dangerous for the U-boats to surface or even to stay near the surface for very long, so at least that wasn't a problem for the moment.

That was what we thought anyway, until, the fourth day out, on a day that should have been safe, our convoy was rocked by two explosions, one right after the other. The call went out to general quarters and we scrambled—carefully because of all the ice—to our battle stations. There didn't seem to be any way I could climb up to the crow's nest, so I was in the sonar room and blind to what was going on outside. But I could feel it when the PC's engines heated up and we lurched forward in search of the U-boats responsible for the attack—and the ships that had just been hit, and, hopefully, any survivors.

I wasn't in the sonar room long, though—there was already an operator in there, and I was just the backup—because they needed help tying off survivor nets on the side of the ship so we'd be ready in case there were survivors who could climb aboard under their own power, and fewer we'd have to lift out of the lifeboats.

My fingers froze as soon as I got out on the deck. My face froze. Everything froze. Guys were slapping themselves to keep some feeling in their faces, clapping their hands to keep some feeling in their fingers as they loaded the guns and prepared the detonators in the depth charges—and as we tied off survivor nets and flung them down the sides of the ship.

We inched our way back on the frozen deck, holding tight on to safety lines to keep from slipping and to keep from getting tossed over. The PC was pounded by waves as we gave chase to a U-boat we couldn't see in a desperate push to get there before they could fix their sights on another ship and take that one out, too. It was a good thing the storm had pushed the ships in the convoy out of formation, making it harder for the wolf pack to find their next target.

"Prepare to fire depth charges!" The order blasted out of the squawk box. The sonar must have homed in on a U-boat, and we must have been getting close. I braced myself—we all did—when the order came to launch, and then we held our breath and counted as the depth charges were flung forward and to starboard, then sank. One thousand one, one thousand two, one thousand three . . .

The explosions lifted our boat out of the water and then slammed us back down hard. A couple of guys fell and slid down the icy deck until somebody else caught them and pulled them to safety.

No debris came up, and no oil slick, no evidence that we'd scored a hit on the U-boat. I thought we'd turn in the direction of the ships that had gotten hit—the storm had lightened up enough and visibility had increased through what was now just a light snow so we could see the twin spirals of smoke rising off the damaged vessels—but Lieutenant Talley ordered us farther out in pursuit of another U-boat instead.

"What if there are survivors?" Straub said. I could tell he was exhausted from loading and reloading the heavy depth charges. "We can't just let them drown."

Our ship plunged forward, following whatever route the sonar operator said. Rumor had it that there were a dozen U-boats in the wolf pack plaguing the convoy.

"If we don't chase off that wolf pack, there will be a lot more survivors who'll need saving," another sailor answered. "Can't do anything about them right now."

I thought Straub was going to start crying. Instead, he started cursing like I'd never heard him curse before.

"It's just not right," he muttered when he ran out of cusswords.

Nobody had time to answer him this time because we got the order to fire again—depth charges and forward deck gun. Without being ordered to go there, I decided I needed to be up on the observation platform, even with the ocean as rough as it was, and the snow still swirling, and the ice still coating everything on board.

I cautiously made my way up, just in time for the second U-boat to come into view and make an easy target for our deck gun. We fired round after round and scored hit after hit until I was sure it was going to explode and sink.

But before that happened, yet *another* U-boat came up beside it. I saw the periscope and shouted down to the bridge. Lieutenant Talley ordered evasive action and also ordered us to fire away in the direction of the third U-boat.

I wondered if we'd blundered into the middle of that whole U-boat wolf pack, and if we would find ourselves surrounded, sitting ducks, caught in a torpedo cross fire. Lieutenant Talley must have been worrying about the same thing because before I knew it we were hightailing it out of there and back to join up with the convoy.

The U-boats didn't try to follow us—probably too busy tending to the sub—or subs—we'd hit so bad.

Twenty minutes later we approached what was left of the two bleeding ships in our convoy, which wasn't much at all, but we were still hoping there were survivors.

But there weren't—at least none still in lifeboats or in the water. One of the corvettes was already there when we arrived, but we could tell by the looks on the faces of the crew that there wasn't anybody left to save. They were staring helplessly around them at the debris. The ships were already gone. As we pulled alongside the corvette, I realized that a lot of what looked like debris from a distance wasn't that at all. It was bodies.

We all just stood where we were, as if we were frozen ourselves. I had never seen anything so horrible, but I couldn't close my eyes, couldn't look away. I felt faint. I wasn't breathing. I told myself to breathe. To just keep breathing, keep breathing, keep breathing. But through that deep breath, I felt tears on my cheeks, and I was glad I was far enough above the rest of the crew that nobody could see or hear.

In the distance, back where we'd chased the U-boats, more explosions ripped the horizon. One of the destroyers had turned back and was shelling the last-known place the wolf pack had been. We figured the Germans were long gone, but at least we'd managed to chase them off, away from the convoy—for now.

The order came for us to abandon the bodies from the sunken ships, and most of the guys on board wanted nothing more than to get moving again. Sitting still, even in the remnants of an early winter storm and in heavy waves, made us an easy target. But Lieutenant Talley told us we were going to pick up as many of the dead men as we could in the next half hour and give them a proper sea burial before we caught up with the convoy. The Royal Navy corvette captain, once he heard what we were up to, gave the same order.

It was sadder than anything, paddling out in our lifeboats to pull all those poor men out of the ocean. The boats filled quickly. Transferring the bodies back to the ship took forever. The survivor nets I'd helped tie on were useless, except for us, the PC crew, to drag ourselves back on board once the half hour was up.

There were still bodies left, but we couldn't risk staying any longer. The guy who'd replaced me on the observation platform was already seeing periscopes everywhere he looked—none of which turned out to be periscopes. But that was how scared and anxious and vulnerable we all were.

The sea burials took a long time, too. By the end, Lieutenant Talley didn't have to read the Bible passage and the prayer. He had them both memorized and could recite them by heart.

For the next week, all our days and nights were the same. The wolf pack probed our defenses constantly, unless the weather turned too ugly, and sometimes attacked, firing their torpedoes at the vulnerable underbellies of heavy, lumbering cargo ships and sometimes getting spotted by us first. If that happened, the chase was on, our PC hammering through the waves to catch up to a U-boat before it could get away, either by diving and sneaking off before we could lock in with our sonar, or else coming up and running away at surface speed, which was faster than ours. They wouldn't stand and fight since our deck guns were a lot more powerful—unless they were damaged, like what happened on our first voyage, coming back up the East Coast.

We didn't catch any, but we might have damaged a few. The same with the corvettes and the other PCs. The destroyers launched a lot of long-range shots that we were sure ran off a number of U-boats, but we couldn't tell if they ever hit anything directly.

Nobody slept more than an hour or two at a time. There was just too much ocean to cover, and too many ships to protect, and too many menacing U-boats, and too few of us.

CHAPTER 22

One evening, Straub and I and a bunch of other guys were in the mess, just off the dogwatch, waiting for dinner. The ocean was calm for once, so the cooks were able to muster up a real hot meal for us, and one that we'd all get to hold down since nobody was seasick. And since the ship wasn't getting bounced around on choppy seas, we didn't have to worry about everything sliding off the tables, even with the fiddle boards up. It had gotten warmer out, too, temperatures in the fifties, where just a couple of days before we were practically in the middle of an ice storm.

On the downside, we were all pretty much falling asleep just sitting there waiting on the chow to be ready. I felt a thud on my forehead and woke right up—and realized I'd slumped so far forward that my head had hit the table.

"Good thing there wasn't a fork sticking up there," Straub said, though I wasn't sure how he could have seen what just happened with his eyes opened to a couple of narrow slits.

I lifted my cup of cold coffee and drank some to wake myself up. "Wonder how Woody's doing," I said.

"Yeah, I wonder, too," said Straub. "Haven't seen him in probably three whole days. You think he's all right?"

"I guess so," I said. "All those snipes down there in the engine room, they're all pretty tight with one another. Especially since Big Carrot got killed."

"They didn't get a replacement for him, either. Just promoted a guy. So they're all pulling extra duty," Straub said. "I don't think they mind, though."

The cooks brought out steaming pots of, well, something we decided was supposed to be beef stew. There did seem to be chunks of meat floating around in there, bumping into the occasional canned pea or carrot. And there was a lot of green stuff that could have been seaweed. Or colored moss. But we ate it, grateful for a calm ocean, and washed it down with more coffee.

"Want to go see him?" I asked Straub when we finished.

"Who, Woody?" he said. "They'd throw us right out of there. They don't like anybody invading their cave. You know that."

"Maybe it's more relaxed with the new chief motor machinist's mate," I said.

Straub shrugged. "Worth a shot. I mean, I'd hate for Woody to think we're not still his pals and all."

So we made our way back through the bowels of the ship to the engine room, and, as it turned out, nobody said anything to us. They just stared at us when we came in, as if we were aliens from another planet. Maybe it was the deafening noise of all the machinery necessary to turn and control the two giant screws that worked the propellers. Maybe it was the fact that most of the snipes hadn't seen daylight, or anybody besides their fellow grease-smeared snipes, for a couple of days. Or maybe they were just as tired as the rest of us, as desperate for a good, long sleep, and knew they weren't going to get it for weeks to come.

Straub and I waved, taking the friendly approach, and then we went looking for Woody in their sleeping quarters, which was where we found him, asleep in his bunk, snoring, though we could barely hear him over the din from the main engine room on the other side of the bulkhead.

We were just about to wake him when the squawk box blasted the call to general quarters. Woody sat up so fast that he bonked his head on the bunk above him, like in a cartoon. It should have been triced up since nobody was in it, but apparently they were looser about those sorts of things in the engine room.

We shouted hi and good-bye to Woody, who seemed confused to see us, or maybe it was from hitting his head, then we turned to race back to our stations. But something stopped me. I turned to look at Woody again. He was rubbing his head but grinning at me, which struck me as odd.

"You okay?" I asked.

"Oh yeah, sure," Woody said. "This isn't anything. Down here, you hit your head all the time on stuff. Gotta have a hard head to get by."

I should have already been gone. We must have spotted a U-boat and were about to give chase, but I still held back. "Why were you grinning like that?" I asked.

"I don't know," Woody said, looking sheepish. "I just saw that you and Straub came down to visit, and it occurred to me that I ain't ever had friends like you guys before. That's all."

I smiled. "Yeah," I said. "Me too." And then I took off for my duty station and Woody took off for the engine room.

I turned to wave to him for some reason, but I was too late. He was already gone.

Good weather and ocean for eating in the mess was bad weather and ocean for eluding the wolf pack. Once we made it to our stations, Straub and I joined everybody else scanning the horizon for ships on fire. Sonar had picked up something that might've been a U-boat and we were racing toward the spot, practically flying over the waveless sea. It was night, but there was a half-moon and enough light to see the shape of a couple of the cargo ships lumbering forward off to starboard.

We'd had a run of false soundings on sonar the past couple of days and I was beginning to think this might be one more, but then the order came to prepare the depth charges, and the PC slowed. Straub and his depth charge crew went to work, while I helped with shells for the deck gun. I wished I was on the observation platform instead, because while I trusted the other guys, I was pretty sure I was better at spotting U-boats in open water, or even sometimes just having a feeling, a sense, for where one might be, even if there was nothing to actually see.

Lieutenant Talley ordered them to launch the depth charges, and we all braced ourselves for the aftershock. Spouts of water shot up and caught the moonlight. For a second it was actually beautiful. And then the concussion jolted us up out of the water and slammed us back down. Guys staggered, slammed into rails, fell on the deck. The usual. And then another depth charge went off even deeper and it happened again. And then a third depth charge even deeper.

I was picking myself up and back into position by the forward gun when the water next to the ship started frothing and churning. An oil slick formed nearby, coming from below the surface where we'd either hit a U-boat or they were trying to convince us we had. Lieutenant Talley ordered the engine room to back the ship off a little way, and we trained the forward gun at the still-churning water.

We didn't have to wait long before the bow of a U-boat broke through, and then the forward deck, then their deck gun, obviously damaged and half off the mount, then the tower, also damaged. Only half the sub managed to surface. So we'd hit it after all! Guys on our ship cheered until Chief Kerr ordered everybody to shut up and grab small arms.

We kept the forward gun aimed at the U-boat tower. Guys with weapons crouched behind cover with their guns aimed there, too, where the Germans would climb out—if they were still alive, and if they were going to surrender.

So we waited like that. Hardly breathing. Minutes passing. Knowing we couldn't stay like that long because another U-boat in the wolf pack could be lining up to fire a torpedo at us at any time.

"How long you think Lieutenant Talley's gonna wait?" the guy next to me asked.

"I say we go ahead and open fire. Sink this U-boat and get the heck out of here," said another guy.

"But they could still be alive in there. Some of them probably are. Wouldn't you think?" asked the first guy.

"So what if they are?" said the second guy. "What are we going to do with them? We can't take on any prisoners, can we? Can't slow down the convoy just for something like that."

Nobody answered him, because nobody could know the answer.

After five more long minutes that felt like an hour, a German climbed out of the tower and down onto the sloping deck of the U-boat. Another followed. Then several more. They pulled an inflatable raft out with them, looking at us nervously the whole time.

"They're probably waiting for us to start shooting," somebody said. "The way they'd do it to us if the situation was reversed."

We kept guns aimed at the U-boat. Lieutenant Talley and the other officers were on the bridge. He shouted something to the German submariners, but none of them answered. They inflated their boat, still keeping one eye on us to see what we would do, but not asking permission for anything, not saying anything, and then they climbed on board and began paddling away—away from the U-boat and away from our PC.

"What the heck is this?" Straub asked. I hadn't seen him come over to where I was stationed. "We're just letting them get away?"

"It's not like they can do anything," I said. "Except wait to be rescued by another U-boat."

"I say we start shooting," a guy in the forward gun crew snarled.

"Nah," somebody else said. "Lieutenant Talley's going to let them get far enough away, and then he's going to sink their sub. And anybody else on board who didn't come out."

"You gotta figure they're all dead down there, or they'd have come out, too," Straub said.

"I hope that's it," I said. I didn't want to think about men still alive on the U-boat when we fired on it, if that's what Lieutenant Talley was actually planning.

We never got the chance to find out, though, because suddenly the whole world was ripped apart by an enormous explosion—and we were in the middle of it, thrown off our feet, our ship swallowed up in flames.

CHAPTER 23

I don't know if I blacked out, or if I was just so confused by the blast that I didn't know where I was at first. There was smoke everywhere, and everything seemed to be leaning. I was lying down, a sharp pain in one of my legs. Everything was muted, like being underwater. I could still hear guys yelling, someone screaming, but they sounded really far away. Then the boat shook with a second explosion below-decks, and I felt myself tossed again and slammed into something metal—the bridge. I pulled myself up to a sitting position and rubbed my eyes. It was hard to see. I wished I had some water to throw on my face. I blinked and blinked. There was more yelling. There were guys staggering around me. I could see them dimly. My hearing was coming back, too. Someone was screaming—I crawled toward the sound, more feeling my way through the smoke than seeing where I was going at times.

But when I got to him, the screaming stopped. I held his hand and wiped his face clean. His eyes were closed, clenched tightly shut. He'd been hurt really bad. I couldn't even recognize him. But as dazed as I was, I just didn't want him to be alone, even though there wasn't anything I could do for him. There wasn't anything anybody could do. I said a prayer.

That's where I was when Straub found me, still sitting there, cross-legged, holding the dead man's hand. "Come on, Danny," Straub said, taking hold under my arms and lifting me up. "We have to get off the ship. It's going down."

I couldn't put any weight on my wounded leg. When I looked down I saw a jagged piece of metal that had stabbed into my thigh. For some reason I barely felt it, even though I could tell it went in pretty deep. I reached for the metal, but Straub stopped me. "You're in shock. Don't pull it out. You'll bleed too much. You just have to leave it until we get on the lifeboat. We'll get something to bandage you up there."

I couldn't speak, so I just nodded as he half carried me across the sloping deck. Some members of the crew were lying on the deck, not moving. Others were busy grabbing supplies, weapons, medical kits, blankets, radio equipment.

"There's just the one lifeboat," Straub said. "The other one got destroyed. We're all going to have to get in. I don't know how many guys are left."

I struggled to say a name but could barely get it out. I must have inhaled a lot of smoke in the explosion. "Woody?"

Straub wouldn't look at me. He just kept going to the side of the ship.

"What about Woody?" I asked, though it felt as if something was tearing inside my throat.

Straub shook his head. "The second explosion. It was the engine room. Nobody could get down there to help them."

We were at the rail now, and other members of the crew helped Straub lower me into the lifeboat. Chief Kerr was there giving orders, though his face was burned. He had them lay me in the bow, took a look at my leg, and ordered a guy sitting nearby to make sure nobody bumped into me.

I squeezed my eyes closed as tight as I could. I never wanted to open them again. I didn't want to see anymore. I didn't want to hear anymore. I didn't want to know anymore.

But it didn't help. Instead, I saw a picture of Woody in my mind, that last time, just before everything happened, down in the engine room, grinning, telling me he'd never had pals like me and Straub, and me telling him the same.

Our ship didn't give up easy. We'd seen cargo ships that got torpedoed go down in minutes, but our PC held on for a long time, as if refusing to quit until every member of the crew who was still alive could climb or be carried onto the lifeboat. There were so many of us crammed on it that it was hard to believe we'd lost anybody in the attack. But I knew we had. I'd seen them on the deck. And I knew no one had escaped from the engine room. Lieutenant Talley was dead, too.

Chief Kerr did a count once we were all settled, guys practically sitting on top of one another. There were thirty of us. The lifeboat was designed to hold twenty.

We finally shoved off from the ship, guys who were able paddling hard to get some distance in case there was another explosion, and to avoid the danger of a whirlpool pulling us under with it when the ship went down.

Chief Kerr was going man to man to check on injuries. One side of his face looked like burnt hamburger, but he didn't seem to even notice. When he got to me he pulled a roll of gauze, sulfa packets, a needle and thread, and a syringe out of a medical kit.

"Two of you boys hold him down," he ordered the guys squeezed in next to me. He didn't hesitate, just immediately stabbed me in the arm with the syringe. "This is morphine. It'll help you not feel too much."

He waited a few minutes, then turned his attention to the metal shard sticking out of my leg. It was maybe the size of his hand, but it was impossible to tell how much was buried.

"It's gotta come out," he said, and once again didn't hesitate. He pulled quickly and the metal slid right out. I threw up from the pain as blood gushed from the wound. Chief pressed gauze over it and held it there as tight as he could, which hurt almost as bad as when he pulled out the metal shard. I thought I was going to throw up again and I struggled to get away, but the two guys kept their tight hold on me and wouldn't let me up.

Chief pulled back the gauze and coated the wound with sulfa powder—"This'll help with any infection," he said— and then, when the bleeding let up enough, busied himself putting in stitches to close the cut.

He grinned at me when he finished. "There," he said. "Good as new."

"Thanks, Chief," I muttered. And then I blacked out again.

When I regained consciousness, the lifeboat was rocking side to side, and a steady spray was coming over and drenching us. The waves had picked up, and the sky was dark gray. Straub helped me sit and gathered a blanket tighter around me to keep me warm and at least somewhat dry.

"Here," he said, holding up a small cup of water. "You need to drink. Chief says we have to ration everything but that you get extra water since you lost a lot of blood."

I drank slowly. My tongue felt so thick in my mouth, swollen from smoke or from dehydration—I didn't know which. Maybe both.

When I finished I felt even thirstier than before, but Straub said that was going to have to be it for now. "Don't know when somebody will find us," he said. "We thought one of the PCs would come back for us, but maybe they don't know where we are. The radio worked for a little while and then stopped."

I could only nod. And fight off the tears that were pressing against the backs of my eyes, threatening to pour out like somebody opening a faucet. I immediately started thinking about Woody, and what happened to him and the rest of the engine room crew. He'd been my friend since the very first day I showed up for the navy.

Straub must have been able to read my face. "I can't stop thinking about him, either," he said, patting me on the shoulder. "And Lieutenant Talley. And the rest of them, too. We lost half the crew."

"Was it a torpedo?" I managed to ask.

Straub shook his head. "Chief doesn't think so. He says the Germans—the officers, I guess, or whoever stayed below while the rest of the crew left on their inflatable lifeboat—they blew up their own U-boat, and that's what sank our ship." He shook his head as if he just couldn't believe it.

"They blew themselves up so they could sink our ship and kill all of us," he said. "It wasn't a torpedo. It was a suicide."

CHAPTER 24

Nobody from the convoy came back for us that day. A guy named Diego got the radio working again, and we were able to send out a distress signal and our location, but then it died for good a little while later and we didn't have any more contact with the world.

"Just have to try to keep to the shipping lane as best we can," Chief said. "We can navigate by the stars when it's night."

Even though I was still feeling numb from the morphine, I could tell he was in a lot of pain when he spoke from the way he couldn't stop clenching his jaw. Saltwater spray must have stung his burnt face, but he made sure to look away from the crew whenever it got too bad.

Chief and a couple of guys did an inventory of what we had on the lifeboat and it wasn't much: the first-aid kit, a flare pistol, a couple of hand pumps, buckets for bailing, tarps, binoculars, some fishing lines but no bait. The men who had weapons had brought them on board. And we had enough water cans to last us a couple of days if we were careful. And enough rations for that long, too—hardtack and biscuits and several cans of peaches and that was about it.

"Won't be able to make it long on this, Chief," Diego said.

Chief Kerr didn't answer, and for the next several hours everybody sat quietly, hardly talking to one another. I was in a kind of stupor from the drugs but still couldn't stop thinking about Woody and the other guys we'd just lost. It was like losing my dad all over again, with that hollow feeling inside of me, like something big was missing and I knew I'd never get it back.

A couple of times I saw tears streaming down Straub's cheeks, but he wasn't making any noise. No crying sounds or sniffling or anything like that. Just the tears. And he wasn't the only one.

The waves got rough that night and salt water sprayed over everybody as we huddled together for warmth. Once the sun had set, the temperature plunged, and everybody got chilled and stayed that way. Several got seasick and threw up over the side.

I lay there, shivering, as I stared up at the sky. A half-moon hung there, surrounded by stars, and it was beautiful, but at the same time almost seemed to be mocking us in our misery.

Chief Kerr stirred near the bow and pulled himself up so he was standing over us. Maybe he sensed that we were all slipping into a dark place. Maybe he worried that we would give up hope too quickly.

"Grab those buckets, some of you men," he said. "Start bailing. Five-minute shifts, then hand your bucket to the next man."

Water kept sloshing over the sides as the waves rocked us harder for a couple of hours. But at least there was something to do. Nobody slept, not even me, and deep into the night the morphine started to wear off and the pain set in. My leg throbbed and felt hot to the touch. I must have moaned, because Straub noticed.

"Chief, Danny needs more meds," he said. Chief Kerr nodded to the crew member who was holding the first-aid kit, and he climbed over several guys, squeezed in next to me, and gave me another shot of morphine. I didn't feel anything else the rest of that first night.

Just before dawn the ocean got calm again, and as the sun climbed in the sky we dried out and warmed up. Guys who'd been sitting with their legs stretched out bent their knees and drew their legs in so that the men who'd been cramped up for the past few hours could have their turn to stretch out.

Another guy and me near the bow were the only ones who'd been lying down. I felt guilty and so pulled myself up to a seated position. The other guy—Donaldson—couldn't do that because he had died during the night.

I didn't realize it until Donaldson's buddy, who'd been holding him the whole time, broke down. "Easy, son," Chief Kerr said in as kind a voice as I'd ever heard him use. "At least he isn't suffering."

I wanted to pull myself away from Donaldson's body and felt myself trembling—from the cold, and from the terrible realization that I'd been lying next to someone who had been dead for hours.

Diego led us all in saying the Lord's Prayer, and then they eased Donaldson's body over the side and let him go.

Probably to distract us all from the deep sadness that hit everybody again, Chief ordered the morning's rations, which amounted to a mouthful of hardtack and a couple of swallows of water. Straub tried to give me his, but I wouldn't let him.

"I think I'm better," I said, which might have been true. My leg wasn't burning as much, and the pain hadn't come all the way back as the morphine wore off. I decided I would wait as long as I could before asking for any more.

"Okay, men," Chief Kerr said, struggling to stand in the bow so he could see us all while he spoke. "I should have set this up last night, but we were all feeling pretty low from losing our shipmates." He paused, and added, "From losing our friends."

He paused again and ground his teeth as it looked like a wave of pain passed over him from his burnt face. Then he continued. "I'll be designating all you men for two-hour watches throughout the day and night. Just because we're no longer on our ship doesn't mean there's no danger from U-boats, or from a stray freighter that might come up on us and not know we're here. It's happened plenty of times before—that the ship somebody thinks is coming to their rescue ends up doing just the opposite. And if you haven't noticed, we're being followed."

Several guys jumped up to look off the stern. I swiveled around and pulled myself up to look, too, and saw a half dozen black fins in the water behind us.

Sharks.

"The good news is that means there are other fish in the water and we might luck into catching some," Chief said. "Meanwhile, if you're the praying kind, you'll want to be praying for rain. We'll open the tarps to catch as much as we can. It'll be salty but not as salty as seawater. We can strain it through our shirts, and we'll use a couple of the buckets to hold it in. We can hold on without food for a couple of weeks. Can't go but a couple of days without water.

"We also need to take extra care of the weapons on hand and protect our ammunition. I want every weapon cleaned twice a day and ammo properly stored."

Right away I could tell guys felt a little better. Once again they had a job to do, whether it was keeping watch, praying for rain, or cleaning the weapons we had on board. Everybody seemed to sit up straighter, and conversations broke out here and there as guys for the first time started talking about what had happened the day before with the U-boat, and about our friends who we'd lost.

For the next couple of hours, sharks kept bumping the boat and that gave us something to talk about, too. Could a shark do serious damage to the lifeboat? Should we try to shoot them? Nobody seemed to have any clear answers, but that didn't stop everyone from discussing it for the next couple of hours.

Straub didn't talk, though. He'd started out doing everything he could to take care of me, to make sure I was comfortable, even to the point of giving up his rations if I'd let him. But now, as the day wore on, he grew quieter. I didn't have much energy to try to get him to talk, and I got quieter, too, but in a different way than him. I was wounded in my leg. He seemed to be wounded in his heart.

The sun had been a blessing when it first came up—thawing us out, drying us off, giving us hope that somebody might see us and we might be rescued. But as the sun rose higher and the day got hotter, we were all soon parched and counting down the hours until our next water ration, which wouldn't be until sundown.

Chief Kerr ordered the cans of peaches opened that night and we each got a couple of slices. And a small sip of the peach juice. Nothing had ever tasted so good to me—to all of us, judging by the slurping and smacking sounds the guys were making. The last ones got to stick their tongues in the cans and lick the sides. The rest of us just looked on with envy, wishing it was us.

And that was just the second day.

The days that followed got worse and worse. First the cold, cold nights, the rough ocean, waves rocking us, salt water spraying us, guys trembling and moaning from the bone-deep chill. Then the heat of the climbing sun. It dried up the salt water but sucked all the moisture out of our skin, which got sunburned, and cracked, and then, the next night, if the waves picked up again and water splashed over us, turned painful. So painful on some of the men that they started crying, only after a few days no tears came. None at all.

And the sharks kept circling, still occasionally bumping the bottom of the lifeboat, their dorsal fins visible in the daytime, shadows at night. They stayed close, letting us know they were there, biding their time, patiently waiting.

CHAPTER 25

The fifth night it started raining and somebody actually shouted, "Well, hallelujah!"

Except for Donaldson, we hadn't lost anybody else on the boat, and every one of us turned our faces to the sky, opened our mouths, and stuck out our tongues to try to drink the rain.

After a few frustrating minutes of that, we got organized and spread out the tarps and let the rainwater roll down to one end and into a bucket. Once that bucket was full—which took at least an hour—one guy pulled his shirt off and they used it to strain the water into another bucket, meanwhile continuing to collect as much rainwater as possible in the middle of the tarps.

"Double water rations tonight," Chief announced, and everybody cheered. The water had a strong briny taste, but it was still water and nowhere near the salt of the ocean, so it helped with the crippling thirst that was making our tongues swollen and our lips blistered.

The rain only lasted a few hours, but our luck still held that night when a school of mackerel swam close and one of the guys was somehow, miraculously, able to grab one and throw it into the boat.

At first I thought there would be a feeding frenzy, men literally taking bites out of the fish before scaling it and cleaning it or anything. But once again, Chief Kerr stepped in.

"Everybody will get a bite," he said. "But not like this. We need to use everything. Head, guts, everything. This is more important to us as bait than it is as food."

I volunteered to clean the fish since I'd been doing it all my life, plus it was something to do to take my mind off this fear that had been growing in me—the possibility that we wouldn't ever get rescued, and that my mom would never know what happened to me.

They had to pass the fish to me, and one of the knives, since I couldn't move with my bad leg, and there was no room for anybody to move on the boat anyway. I made short work of it, cutting the meat into bite-size pieces for guys to pass around. It was tough to eat, but we were already out of hardtack and biscuits and peaches—had been for two days—so anything was better than nothing.

Chief Kerr passed out the fishing lines and I baited those, too, with the intestines. Guys caught two more fish that night, and we feasted again the next day. I felt a little better after that, and a little more hopeful. For a while.

Straub still wasn't speaking, but after another couple of days, neither were the rest of us. My leg felt okay, but I knew I couldn't put any weight on it even if I tried to stand. At least there didn't seem to be an infection. Maybe the nightly drenching in salt water helped with that, though it was terrible on the rest of my body—the rest of all our bodies. Sores broke out on our skin, on our faces, on our tongues, inside our mouths.

We kept catching fish but never enough to make our hunger really go away. Enough to keep us alive, I guess. And there was some moisture in the meat, which also helped. But we desperately needed another rain.

We didn't get one, though. Not for a while. After eight days we even tried peeing in the buckets—not that anybody had much pee in them. Some didn't have any. But it was undrinkable, even with the severe thirst we all had. Worse than drinking seawater. And seawater, we'd always been told, would pretty quickly kill you if you drank it and kept drinking it.

That didn't stop me from thinking about it, though. Even fantasizing about it. Just a sip. What could possibly happen if I took just one little sip? Surely it would help some. Even a little relief from the terrible thirst would be something.

A guy named Benjy beat me to it and immediately wished he hadn't, because he gagged for a long time and threw up the bite of fish he'd just had—the only thing he would have to eat all that day. Nobody was sympathetic. Nobody said anything except to call him an idiot.

When he stopped gagging, Benjy went after Conner, the sailor who'd called him that, the two of them sprawling over other guys, who punched them both until Chief Kerr roared at everybody to knock it off—or else he'd be throwing bodies to the sharks.

Just to make sure, Chief climbed over to where the two men were fighting and grabbed their collars and pulled them apart.

"This is not going to happen on my boat!" he yelled in their faces, shaking them like they were a couple of little kids. And like little kids they immediately calmed down. Neither one would look at him, or at the rest of us. Chief shoved them back to their places.

Somebody must have bumped into him during the melee because when he stood back up to lecture us more I saw that Chief's face was bleeding where he'd been burned. A lot.

Benjy took off his shirt and handed it to Chief Kerr. Chief took it and just stared at the shirt for a minute. He must have felt the blood oozing down his cheek because he put his hand there and it was covered with blood when he pulled it away. He didn't use Benjy's shirt, though. He handed it back.

"Put it on," he said. "You won't last long in this sun without it. Or tonight, either." He shook his head. "Here's the thing, men. We stick together, we survive this. We work together, we survive this. We take care of one another, we survive this. It's as simple as that."

"Sorry, Chief," said Benjy, putting his shirt back on.

"Sorry, Chief," said Conner, the sailor who'd called Benjy an idiot.

"I don't want to hear 'sorry,'" Chief Kerr said. "I just want this to be the end of it."

And it was. There wasn't any more fighting after that. Guys might say a cross word now and then to one another, but nobody wanted to get on Chief's bad side. And probably we were all growing too weak to fight or even disagree much as well.

The next few days were just like the ones before—freezing nights, rough waves, sharks bumping the lifeboat, blistering days. The only happy moments were when somebody caught a fish—usually mackerel or sea bass—and we all got to eat and satisfy our water craving from the wet meat, at least a little. Once somebody caught a small shark and we tried to eat that, but it was too tough. We chewed and chewed but didn't have any spit in our mouths to soften it up, or strength in our jaws to wear down the meat enough to even swallow it. A couple of guys tried drinking blood but that was almost impossible to get out, and it ended up making them sick.

I could feel myself growing weaker, and sadder—about Woody and the others who died, and about the possibility that we might never be found and I might never see my mom or Danny or home again. I prayed we would be rescued, and I prayed that if we weren't, that Mama and Danny would somehow find out what happened to me, and would know that I loved them all the way to the end.

And then, just when we were probably all giving up hope, it rained again. Only this time it wasn't a rough, stormy rain, but almost like a warm spring rain, though it was now late October. We filled all our buckets this time, not keeping any of them empty for bailing. We drank more than we had in two weeks, and then we filled the buckets again.

"Maybe it's a sign," Benjy said. "Maybe we'll be rescued soon."

"Yeah," Conner said. "Bound to happen."

Since the fight, Benjy and Conner seemed to have become friends, somehow.

We all wanted to believe them, of course. It was just that nobody actually did. Heck, they didn't even believe it themselves; they were just talking was all.

CHAPTER 26

The next day, Diego, who was on watch, saw something on the horizon. A speck. Everybody jostled everybody else as we all tried to get in a position to see. Chief Kerr pulled out the binoculars and studied it. Waves erased whatever it was, then revealed it again, then erased it again. Finally, he figured it out.

"It's the Germans," he said, handing the binoculars to the guy beside him so he could look, too.

"What Germans?" Diego asked.

"The ones in the inflatable life raft," Chief said. "The ones we let paddle away. Guess they didn't paddle far enough. Or maybe they just managed to paddle themselves in a big circle."

Over the next couple of hours, the life raft slowly came closer. And as it did, I felt anger burning me up inside. These were the Germans who kept us distracted while their officers down below set explosives in their U-boat—the explosives that killed Woody. The explosives that killed half our crew.

I wasn't the only one getting angry.

"We ought to kill them," Straub said. They were the first words he'd spoken in a couple of days. "I hope the wind or waves will keep pushing them closer to us, pushing us closer to them, pushing us together so we can shoot every last one of them."

Chief Kerr stood up in the bow and glared at Straub. Other men were nodding at what he'd just said, and Chief glared at them, too.

"They're unarmed," he said. "You all saw them when they paddled off in their inflatable. They barely had any supplies with them."

"What do we do, then, Chief?" Straub asked, suddenly the most talkative man on the boat. "What if they want some of our rations? Some of our water?"

"We don't have enough," Diego said. "We can't share with them. We'll all die out here—them *and* us."

"So we shoot them and put them out of their misery," Straub said.

The Germans were maybe a hundred yards away now. Chief Kerr handed out weapons and ammunition to several guys—five rifles and a couple of handguns. "Just in case," he said. "And nobody does anything unless I give the word."

"So what are we going to do with them, Chief?" Benjy asked. "You never said."

"I don't know," Chief Kerr said. "I don't know. But we don't shoot and that's an order."

The Germans were maybe fifty yards away now. There were only half a dozen of them, though there'd been probably twice that many when they left the damaged U-boat and paddled away on their raft. The ocean was growing rougher, rocking us harder, but bouncing them around a lot worse.

"Hold steady," Chief said. "Let them draw next to us, and we'll see what they want."

But Straub wasn't going to wait. He lunged over to Conner, the man closest to him with a rifle, and grabbed it. Then he shoved past a couple of guys to the side of the boat and took aim at the Germans.

"Straub, don't!" I shouted. "What are you doing?"

"Don't touch me," he said. "I'll shoot their boat if anybody touches me."

Chief told the guys to pull back, though there wasn't much space for us to go.

Then he addressed Straub. "Sailor, you need to lower that weapon right now," he barked.

"I can't, Chief," he said. "They killed my friend. They killed all of our friends. This is war. Isn't this what we're supposed to do? Kill the enemy?"

He was crying but kept the rifle aimed at the Germans. They saw what he was doing and all raised their hands in surrender.

"Shooting them won't bring anybody back," Chief said. "You know that. War isn't about killing men. It's about fighting for a cause. These men already surrendered. Don't make yourself a murderer. That's what they do. That's not what we do."

"I don't care," Straub said. "I don't care about anything." He swayed, staggered as a wave rocked the boat, then righted himself. He kept his aim the whole time.

"Straub." It was me speaking, but the sound of my own voice surprised me. "Straub, it's me," I said. "You know Woody was my friend, too. I miss him, too. I miss all the guys, the same as you. We all do. But this isn't the way to fix things."

"Then what is?" he said. "What?"

"I don't know," I said softly. "But those guys over there, those German sailors. You know you could have been one of them. If your parents hadn't left Germany, hadn't come to America, and if you had been born there instead of born here, you could have been one of them. You wouldn't have been a Nazi—I know you wouldn't—but it's gotta be the same there as it is here. You have to follow your orders. Those guys over there that you want to shoot—they were following their orders. They didn't have a choice."

I paused. "If it had been you, you wouldn't have had a choice. So if you shoot them, it would kind of be like shooting yourself, too. Or any one of us."

Straub was crying so hard now that he probably couldn't see anything on the Germans' lifeboat. He lowered the rifle. Somebody grabbed it out of his hands. His legs gave out and he sagged back down into the boat and it was over.

We ended up giving the Germans some of our water and some of our fish. Speaking through one of the Germans who knew a little English—his name was Franz—Chief Kerr managed to get across that they could either stay tied up to us and be taken prisoner when and if we were ever rescued, or they could go back out on their own.

Franz rubbed a hand over his blond crew cut, looked around at the rest of his crew, and said they would stay and be our prisoners. He said they hadn't had any water in three days and hadn't eaten in more than a week.

Chief ordered a couple of the crew to tie their raft to our boat—with about twenty yards between the two boats. He gave them fishing line and a bucket and one of our tarps. "We'll share what we can after this," he said through the translator.

An hour later, after everything calmed down, Chief Kerr made his way over to where Straub and I were. Straub hadn't said anything since giving up the gun. I had my hand on his shoulder to let him know I was there, and that I was his friend no matter what. Crouching next to us, Chief looked hard at Straub until Straub lifted his head.

"Son, what you did was wrong," he said. "An order is an order, and it's your job, your duty, to follow orders. I don't care how bad you're hurt, or how bad you miss your friend, or what those Germans did to us. I don't care about none of that. You understand?"

"Yes, Chief," Straub whispered.

"We all feel the same way. You weren't the only one that wanted to shoot those Germans. But it's not who we are and it's not what we do. It's not the American way. Simple as that."

This time Straub struggled to sit up so he could look at Chief Kerr the way he was supposed to when a petty officer gave an order to a seaman second class.

"I understand, Chief," he said. "And I'm sorry."

Chief Kerr put his hand on Straub's other shoulder and squeezed it gently, the way my dad used to do when he was still with us, when I messed up and Dad needed to set me straight about something.

"Nothing more we need to say about this, then," Chief said. "There's not going to be a report on it. What happens out here in this lifeboat—it stays out here and that's the end of it. I just need you to be strong and be the best sailor you can be until we get rescued. Can I count on you for that?"

"Yes, Chief," Straub said.

After Chief Kerr left, Straub whispered to me, "I don't know what came over me, Danny. I just don't. Except I couldn't stop thinking about Woody down there in the engine room, our brave pal Woody. And the ways he might have died down there. And all the stuff we went through together, you and me and him. And what a good guy he was."

"I know," I said. "It's the same for me. It's the same for all of us. I don't blame you for what you did. Or what you almost did. Nobody does."

Straub nodded. Then he said, "I hate this war."

I almost said "We all do," but I didn't need to. He knew.

Two days later, a navy destroyer spotted us. It was our same convoy, returning to America, so we'd managed to keep close enough to the shipping lane after all. They said they hadn't been able to search for us when our ship sank because while we were fighting one U-boat, there were half a dozen other coordinated U-boat attacks all along the flanks of the convoy. All the PCs and corvettes, and the destroyer, had been busy fighting off the rest of the wolf pack. The battle had gone on for hours, the convoy continuing forward the whole time.

The good news was they had been able to protect most of the cargo ships and deliver them safely to England to support the war effort.

The other good news was they had a surgeon on board the destroyer, and he would be able to operate on my leg.

Straub stayed by my side when they carried me down below. "Don't worry, Danny," he said. "I'll be right here with you. I'll make sure they take good care of you and you make it home okay."

CHAPTER 27

It was the end of October when we finally made it back to the US. They transferred me to a hospital in New York City, which seemed more like a giant warehouse, with rows of white beds that stretched out as far as I could see. There weren't any curtains or anything for privacy, but there also weren't very many guys in there. It was pretty lonely. I asked one nurse why there were so many beds for so few people. She paused for a minute, and then said, "We're not supposed to say, but what they told us was that once we start fighting the Germans over there—in Europe or Africa or France—we're going to need every one of these beds for the casualties they ship back home, and a whole lot more, too."

The rumor was that it would happen any day now—the invasion force finally going over from America to join up with the British and attack the Germans and the Italians somewhere on the other side of the Atlantic.

The thought of this whole warehouse hospital full of casualties made my heart sink. We'd been waiting what felt like forever for the invasion force to be called up, but now that I'd been in battles with the U-boats, and seen what I'd seen, and lost my friends, I couldn't get excited about more war, no matter what we were fighting it for. I knew it had to be done, but I just felt sad. Day after day in the hospital. Sad and growing sadder.

A week after I got there, a couple of navy officers came to see me, each formally shaking my hand as they introduced themselves. I thought they were there to give me a medal or something, but that wasn't it at all.

"Colton Graham?" the shorter one, Lieutenant Frost, asked.

Panic bloomed in my gut. "No, sir. It's Danny Graham."

"No, it isn't," said the tall officer, Lieutenant Ryals. "We know who you are."

"We've been in contact with your mother," said Lieutenant Frost. "Your brother is Danny Graham, and he's at home under her care."

I knew there wasn't any use in pretending, and I realized I didn't care. More than that, I was actually glad they knew. I wanted to go home.

"Did she say how he's doing?" I asked.

"Your brother, Danny?" Lieutenant Frost asked. He actually smiled. "You'll be happy to know he's doing pretty good, according to your mom. He came out of his coma, and he's walking and talking. Moving slow. That's about all we know. Sounds like he might be okay, but you're in a lot of trouble."

Now I was nervous. I swallowed hard. "What kind of trouble?"

Lieutenant Ryals answered. "The kind of trouble you get into with your mother when you run away from home and join the navy when you're thirteen."

Lieutenant Frost added, "In other words, not so much in trouble with the navy as in trouble with your mom. As far as the navy is concerned, a mistake was made. A mistake was discovered. And with you being sent home, a mistake will be corrected."

Straub showed up the next day to visit me. I was in physical therapy, trudging up and down a hallway with a walker to build up strength in my hurt leg. The wound had mostly healed, but the doctors said there was a lot of damage to muscles and nerves, and a lot of scar tissue. All I knew was it was hard to stand up for very long and hard to walk without something to hang on to. And they wanted me to be able to walk, or at least sort of walk, before they officially discharged me from the navy.

"Don't you look like an old man!" Straub said when he saw me.

I had to laugh, because I felt like an old man instead of thirteen and a half.

"At least they let you wear pajama pants and not just that gown that you tie in back but your butt sticks out," he said.

"Lucky me," I said.

"You mean lucky *us*," Straub said, shuffling beside me as I kept trudging along that hallway. The sooner I finished the physical therapy, the sooner they'd let me crawl back into my bed.

Straub spent the next half hour filling me in on how everybody was doing, or everybody he'd kept in touch with. They'd divided up what was left of our crew onto several different PCs that had also lost crew members protecting cargo ships on other convoys. Straub and Chief Kerr were assigned to the same ship, and they were heading down to

Norfolk, Virginia, in a couple of days. It was gloomy outside the hospital windows, though that could have been all the dirt and grime caked on the glass.

"Why Norfolk?" I asked. I knew it was a big shipbuilding port, and there was a lot of military stationed there.

"Nobody's saying," Straub said. "But we're all pretty sure this is it. The invasion force. It's finally going to happen. Probably in a couple of weeks, maybe even early November. Wish you could ship out with us."

Straub went on for a while, repeating all the rumors he'd heard, speculating on what everybody thought the Allies ought to do, and when, and how bad we were sure to beat the Germans once we were there—wherever *there* turned out to be. "I'm betting on North Africa," he said. "Lot of people are saying that. Hit the Germans and the Italians there, then cross the Mediterranean and into Italy. Work up to the rest of Europe, up to France. They call that the soft underbelly of Europe, going in that way. Or maybe we'll do that, and go across from England, too. Hit them on two fronts. Everybody's got ideas about it. I'm just ready for it to happen."

I asked what he thought the Donald Duck Navy would be doing. Our ships weren't big enough to carry troops or heavy weapons for bombing enemy defenses from offshore.

"Command vessels, definitely," Straub said. "It's the only thing that makes sense. You got all these destroyers and battleships and transport ships and supply ships, you're gonna need some smaller ships to run around and coordinate it all."

"Who'd you hear that from?" I asked.

He grinned. "Chief Kerr. He told me that. He also told me to tell you he was gonna come by and see you before we shove off, too. He's been busy getting to know the officers and the crew on our new PC. But he said he wanted to check in on you." He paused for a second, and then added, "He knows, by the way—we all know—about how you're not really seventeen, and your real name, and about your brother. Some navy investigators tracked Chief down and asked him a bunch of questions about you, and that's when they told him."

I gulped, wondering if Chief could still make me do push-ups or clean decks even though I wasn't in the navy anymore. I figured he was furious with me.

Straub had to go, but he walked me to my bed from physical therapy first. I was exhausted and could barely drag my legs back under the sheets.

"You take good care of yourself, Colton," he said. "I want you to get all well and out of this place. When we finish up with those Nazis I'll come back here and you and me will go to another baseball game in the spring. Or else maybe I'll come visit you at the Outer Banks. I guess they'll be sending you home now that they know everything."

"I'd like that," I said—meaning the thought of going home to Ocracoke, and the thought of Straub visiting me there when the war was all over.

After Straub left, I drifted off to sleep—something I was doing a lot of in the hospital—and had worrisome dreams about U-boats and silver torpedoes streaking toward our ship. I was on the lookout platform, trying to yell, to warn everybody, but no sound came out.

I woke up in a sweat, tossing and turning, mumbling, vaguely aware that somebody was sitting next to my bed. Whoever it was put a hand on my arm to calm me, and then put a cool cloth on my forehead. A familiar voice, one I hadn't heard in months, said, "It's okay, Colton. You were just having a bad dream, but you're awake now and I'm here with you."

I took away the cloth and opened my eyes, not believing what I was hearing and now seeing:

It was Mama.

I might have cried some before, but now I was practically bawling like a baby as Mama sat there and held on to me until I guess I cried myself dry of tears. Everything seemed to wash over me, lying there with her holding me: how scared I'd been, and how worried about Danny, how guilty I felt for running away like I did, and for hurting her, and for deserting her when she probably needed me the most. How angry I was at the Germans and their U-boats for killing Woody and Lieutenant Talley and so many other guys on my crew—and how much all that anger had taken over the whole inside of me.

Mama just stayed there and kept holding me while I let it all out.

Then she told me, before I could even ask, that Danny was going to be okay—that he was out of his coma, which I already knew, and a lot more. He did have some kind of brain injury, but he was slowly regaining everything they were afraid he might have lost, like the ability to walk on his own, and talk, and feed himself.

"He's such a strong young man," Mama said, sounding a lot softer than I'd heard her sound in years, probably since Dad died. "I believe he'll eventually be all the way back to how he was before the incident."

She told me the navy had contacted her when we got to port and I was transferred to the hospital since she was listed on Danny's enlistment paperwork as next of kin. That was how the truth finally came out. People on Ocracoke took up a collection to buy Mama a bus ticket to come up to New York to see about me.

She stayed for three days but had to go back before I was formally discharged—from the hospital and from the navy. A couple of different officers came by one day—this time to officially chew me out for lying about my age and pretending to be Danny and putting my fellow sailors in harm's way. The one who said that—a captain—was snarling the whole time he talked to me. But the officer who was with him stayed behind when the captain left.

"I read your file," the second officer said. "I don't know what possessed you to enlist, or how you got past everybody, as young as you are and as young as you look, but your chief petty officer went to great pains to let us know what a top-notch seaman you were and that it was an honor for them to serve with you on PC-450."

He tapped a folder he'd been holding, which I guessed contained whatever file the navy had on me. "It says in here that you voluntarily dove into a stormy ocean to save one of your shipmates. And it says without your hard work and your diligence, PC-450 might well have sustained a direct hit on more than one occasion from enemy torpedoes."

He saluted, and I saluted back from my hospital bed. "Fine job, sailor," he said, and then he did an about-face and marched out of the room.

Chief Kerr came in to see me the next day. His face had mostly healed from where it had been burned, but I could still see some scars. He got on me about lying about my age, too, but he couldn't keep a straight face while he was doing it, and finally he just started laughing.

"I knew you were underage, but I had no clue that you were just barely a teenager!" he said. "You got some serious guts, I can tell you that. Some very serious guts! I'm just glad you didn't spill any of those serious guts out on the deck instead of that little scratch you got there on your leg."

"Little scratch!" I exclaimed. "I can barely walk on it, Chief!"

He put his hand on my shoulder and squeezed. "Take it easy, son. Just messing around with you a little bit." He got kind of serious. "You were a good sailor, no matter your name.

I wish I'd had a whole crew of men just like you. Maybe a little older, but just like you other than that."

"Thank you, Chief," I said. "But I don't think we could have had a better crew."

He nodded. "You're right about that, son." He got a far-away look in his eyes and then repeated it. "You're right about that."

A week later I was on a long bus ride back to North Carolina and then a short ferry ride over to Ocracoke. My career in the navy as a subchaser was officially over.

Danny and I were both different after that. Mama said so, and I could see it for myself. Danny had problems remembering things that just happened, like if we'd just had lunch, or if he'd read the newspaper yet that day. He got better over time, so that if you hadn't known Danny before, you wouldn't know that he was sometimes a little behind on everything—answering a question, getting up to go when it was time, cleaning a fish he'd caught. More than once I found him just standing and staring at what was right in front of him, as if he needed to mull over for a minute what he was going to do next before he did it.

My leg healed okay and I didn't have any problems with weakness or balance, except every once in a while. When summer finally came again, Danny and I sat on the porch a lot, in the afternoon shade, watching the surf, or on stormy evenings sitting out there with Mama to watch the lightning dance way out over the dark ocean.

We didn't talk much. Eventually, I told them all about what happened when I left the island, but after that, we were mostly silent. Worried about the war. Worried about what would become of us all. And at the same time thankful we were all alive, and safe, and together again.

I wanted to go to eighth grade, but since I was a whole year behind they decided I would have to finish up the year in seventh grade. I didn't like that much—all the kids seemed so little and so young. But I probably would have felt that same way if I was with my old friends, too. Guess you couldn't go off to war and expect to feel the same about things and people when you came back home.

Some days after school Danny and I corralled our beach ponies and rode them all over the island, over the packed dunes, through the gentle surf, back along the edges of the marsh on the sound side. More and more fishing boats were venturing back out to sea. More and more cargo ships passed without escorts or convoys.

We had never bothered to name our beach ponies, since they didn't actually belong to us, or to anybody. They were just wild and used to being around people and nice enough to let us ride them. I asked Danny what he thought of us giving them names now, though. He considered it for a few minutes, and then said he guessed that would be all right.

He hesitated again, thinking hard about something, and then asked what names I had in mind.

"Woody and Straub," I said.

"Your friends?" Danny asked. "From your ship?"

I nodded. It was funny how I hadn't thought of either one of them that way for a long time after I met them. But besides Danny, I couldn't think of any better friends I would ever have in the world.

AUTHOR'S NOTE

While *Sink or Swim* is a work of fiction, it was inspired in part by the true story of Calvin Graham, who enlisted in the US Navy when he was twelve years old, and at thirteen served on the battleship USS *South Dakota* in the South Pacific in intense fighting with the Japanese. In one memorable and tragic battle, the *South Dakota* took forty-two enemy hits. Thirty-eight men were killed and sixty were wounded, including Calvin Graham, who fell through three stories of the ship's superstructure. Though seriously injured, he crawled through the ship, helping others who had also been wounded. Graham was awarded a Bronze Star and a Purple Heart, but when his mother back home in Texas saw news-reel footage of the battle and recognized her son, she contacted the navy and told them his true age. She had thought he was living with other relatives. Calvin Graham was subsequently sent home, his military career over.

According to the American Veterans Center, as many as 200,000 underage men and women served in the US military during World War II, a number of them as young as fourteen, though Calvin Graham, at twelve, was the youngest. For more of his story, check out author Gilbert King's article in the December 19, 2012, *Smithsonian* magazine, "The Boy Who Became a World War II Veteran at 13 Years Old."

Though twelve-year-old Colton Graham in *Sink or Swim* is a fictional character, the events depicted in the novel—occurring during the Battle of the Atlantic—were all too real. From January to December 1942, German U-boats sank or damaged hundreds of ships and killed around five thousand men and women along the East Coast of the United States and in the Gulf of Mexico, disrupting supply lines, hampering the war effort, and instilling fear in millions of Americans bracing themselves for the terrible coming war in North Africa and Europe against the Axis powers. Many of the cargo and passenger ships attacked by the U-boat fleet went up in explosions and flames within sight of hundreds of people on shore. During the early years of the war, the U-boat wolf packs sank hundreds of other boats crossing the Atlantic to bring desperately needed weapons, food, and other supplies to Great Britain and the Soviet Union under the Lend-Lease Act, which was passed in March 1941.

British Prime Minister Winston Churchill was so concerned about the possibility that the German U-boats would succeed in cutting off the North Atlantic supply line from the US that he wrote, "The only thing that ever really frightened me during the war was the U-boat peril."

Unfortunately, many of the ships sunk by U-boats mentioned in this story actually happened, including the USS *Allan Jackson* on January 18, 1941; the *Atlanta* passenger ship on January 19, 1942; and the USS *Gulfamerica* on April 10, 1942. These are just a few of the many ships that were lost in the Atlantic during the war.

The scene at the Ernest Hemingway house in Key West is also fictional, but the descriptions of the house, the pool, the six-toed cats, and Hemingway's sons, who were living there with their mother at the beginning of the war—while their father, Ernest Hemingway, was living in Cuba and hunting U-boats on his fishing boat—are all true.

Additionally, Lieutenant Commander Eugene McDaniel actually was a commanding officer at the Subchaser Training Center in Miami, Florida, and the stories about him are all true and drawn from historical accounts, as are the descriptions of the Subchaser Training Center itself and the Naval Training Center Great Lakes, where thousands of young navy recruits were sent for their basic training at the start of World War II—and spent countless hours in drills on the Grinder.

Writer Kevin Duffus interviewed eyewitnesses on the Outer Banks for his fascinating article "When World War II was fought off North Carolina's beaches" for the spring 2008 issue of *Tar Heel Junior Historian*, and Michael Graff tells the story of Ocracoke Islanders' encounters with U-boats in an article titled "Graveyard of the Atlantic Museum" in the April 2013 issue of *Our State* magazine. Both were important sources of information for *Sink or Swim*. I highly recommend them for those who would like to read more on the subject. Also helpful in my research were Nathan Miller's *War at Sea: A Naval History of World War II*, Richard Hough's *The Longest Battle: The War at Sea, 1939–45*, and Chris Howard Bailey's *The Battle of the Atlantic: The Corvettes and Their Crews: An Oral History*.

Most important, I could not have written *Sink or Swim*—or learned a fraction of what I now know about patrol crafts, the Donald Duck Navy, navy boot camp, subchaser school, and so much more concerning these unsung heroes—without the help of William J. Veigele's *Patrol Craft of World War II: A History of the Ships and Their Crews*. My thanks to him, and my deep appreciation for his service in the US Navy during World War II and for his years of work to tell the story of all the unnamed PCs and those who served on them.

My friend Rob Jobrack, Lieutenant, USN-retired, who served on the navy's newest class of destroyers, the Arleigh Burke class, and has operated and developed navy surface ship combat since 1984, was kind enough to review the *Sink or Swim* manuscript to help ferret out inaccuracies. Any mistakes that remain are, of course, mine. More importantly, my thanks to Rob for his years of service in the US Navy.

GLOSSARY

aft: the back of a ship

Battle of the Atlantic: A naval campaign that began in 1939 and lasted until 1945. It was German U-boats hunting Allied navies, including the US Navy, the Royal Navy, merchant ships, and others. During the war, U-boats sank 2,779 ships for a total of 14.1 million tons, approximately 70 percent of all Allied shipping losses in all theaters of the war. The worst year was 1942, when more than 6 million tons of shipping were sunk in the Atlantic.

belowdecks: inside the ship

Bluejackets' Manual: handbook issued to all new recruits intended to cover a range of navy procedures, rules, etc.

bowline: a loop-shaped knot that doesn't slip

bridge: the area of the ship from which it's navigated

bulkhead: a wall within the hull of a ship

calisthenics: exercises done without equipment to increase strength and flexibility

commissary: a supermarket for military personnel

corvette: a highly maneuverable armed escort ship

coxswain: sailor who is in charge of the boat and crew

depth charge: a drum filled with explosives that is dropped near a target before it explodes

dogwatch: one of two two-hour watch shifts on a ship, from 4 to 6 p.m. and 6 to 8 p.m., during which crews not on duty eat their main meal of the day

double time: a marching speed

echolocation: process of locating objects by sound waves reflected back from the objects

evasive action: defensive movements to avoid enemy fire or capture

flying bridge: the highest bridge on a ship that has more than one

forecastle: part of the upper deck of a ship in front of the foremast

foremast: the mast nearest the bow of a ship

forward: front part of a ship

general quarters: assigned duty stations for a crew, especially when under attack

Grinder: drill field

head: bathroom on a ship

Hedgehog: antisubmarine weapon

hull: main body of a ship

knot: unit to measure a ship's speed; one knot, or nautical mile per hour, is equal to approximately 1.151 miles per hour

lee: side of a ship away from the wind

Lend-Lease Act: A bill enacted on March 11, 1941, under which the US provided supplies such as food, weapons, oil, etc. to the Allied nations, mainly the UK and the USSR. (Later this included other countries on the Allied side.) In exchange, the US had leases on military bases within Allied territories. It was initially seen as a way to help the Allied forces without actually engaging in war against the Axis. That all changed after the bombing of Pearl Harbor, but the Lend-Lease Act was in effect until September 1945.

liberty: a brief, authorized leave from naval duty

line: name for rope aboard a boat or ship

mess hall: a place similar to a cafeteria where food is served

midwatch: watch shift from 12 to 4 a.m.

milch cows: German submarines sent out to specific points to refuel U-boats

observation platform: Also known as a crow's nest. A fixed platform often attached to the forward mast with protective railing from which an observer with binoculars can look for other ships, especially enemy ships, as well as use signal flags to send messages to other friendly ships.

Pearl Harbor: A naval base in Hawaii that was bombed by the Imperial Japanese Navy on December 7, 1941. This attack marked the US's entry into World War II, with war being declared the next day. Twenty-one ships were sunk or damaged and run aground, including eight battleships and three destroyers. 2,403 men were killed and another 1,178 were wounded.

periscope: a long tube that contains lenses and mirrors and is used to look over or around something, especially by a person in a submarine to see above the surface of the water

pilot house: platform on the bridge

port: left-hand side when facing the front of a ship

safety line: length of rope tied between a person and a ship to prevent falling overboard

shakedown cruise: a voyage that tests a ship's performance before the ship is sent out to sea

sick bay: area on a ship that acts as an infirmary or hospital

Siege of Leningrad: A military attack by the Germans on Leningrad in the USSR. It started on September 8, 1941, and lasted 872 days, ending on January 27, 1944. At this time, Leningrad was the capital of the USSR and the Germans were trying to defeat the country by taking out this one city. It was a major political city, with important military operations and numerous factories based there, plus a huge population. While Leningrad never surrendered, the attack on the city over two and a half years caused incredible destruction and loss of lives—to date, it is the most deadly siege in history. More than 1.5 million people were killed during the siege, most of them women and children, many of them from starvation and disease.

skiff: small boat

skivvies: term for underwear in the navy

sonar: system for detecting objects using sound waves

squawk box: a loudspeaker

starboard: right-hand side when facing the front of a ship

superstructure: the part of a ship above the main deck

survivor net: a net hung over the side of a ship for crew members to climb down to lifeboats if they are forced to abandon ship, or on which survivors from other sinking ships can climb on board a rescue ship from their lifeboats or from the water

U-boat: a shortening of *Unterseeboot*, which means "undersea boat" in German; refers to German submarines

USSR: stands for Union of Soviet Socialist Republics; name of what is now called Russia from 1922 to 1991

wolf pack: a group of submarines working together on a coordinated attack

ACKNOWLEDGMENTS

Many thanks to Kelly Sonnack and Jody Corbett—as much collaborators as wonderful agent and editor. Thanks also to Maeve Norton for her terrific design, Melissa Schirmer for keeping us all on track, and Jody Revenson for her eagle-eye copyediting. And thank you to the rest of the Scholastic team, including Brooke Shearouse, Jana Haussmann, and all the others behind the scenes—from sales to marketing—who were invaluable in bringing *Sink or Swim* to life.

ABOUT THE AUTHOR

Steve Watkins is the author of the novels *Juvie*; *What Comes After*; *Great Falls*; *Down Sand Mountain*, winner of the Golden Kite Award; and the Ghosts of War series, including *The Secret of Midway*, *Lost at Khe Sanh*, *AWOL in North Africa*, and *Fallen in Fredericksburg*.

A former professor of journalism, creative writing, and Vietnam War literature, Steve now runs a nonprofit yoga studio and works with an urban reforestation organization in his hometown of Fredericksburg, Virginia.

Read the Ghosts of War ser

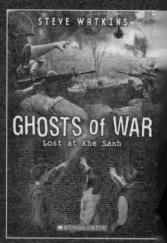

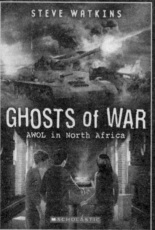

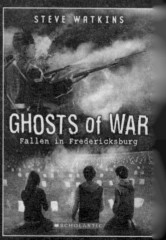

When Anderson, Greg, and Julie discover a trunk fu
old military stuff—and the ghosts that go with it—t
friends find themselves wrapped up in years-old se
that they must unlock before the ghosts disappe
forever, their mysteries unsolved.